I0827973

THE MIDNIGHT TRAIN MURDERS

Jim Keane

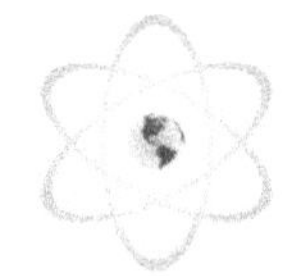

2021, TWB Press
www.twbpress.com

The Midnight Train Murders

Edited by Terry Wright

Cover Art by Terry Wright

ISBN: 978-1-944045-82-1

The Midnight Train Murders

Journalist Russell Carson didn't believe a vampire had murdered passengers on the Metro-North trains any more than he believed Santa Claus was coming to town. However, tabloid readers wanted a story, the more sensational the better, so he'd made up a doozy. He was about to learn that truth was more horrifying than fiction.

After writing for the reputable *Daily Gazette* for twenty years, which covered the Bronx and Westchester, he was now writing for the *National Scrutinizer* because the *Gazette* had fired him for getting a controversial story-fact wrong.

The first three rules of reporting: *accuracy, accuracy, and accuracy.*

Russell remembered when he was a lowly beat reporter on his first assignment: *The Man on the Street Interview.* It took him three hours to get a statement and photograph from one of seven residents standing in front of a Bronx deli in the freezing cold of winter. After that, his outlook on groundbreaking journalism cooled considerably from his optimistic view that he was going to be a great reporter, but he never gave up.

Flash forward to his last day at the *Daily Gazette*.

With the increasing pressure to break the news first, Russell forgot the most essential tenet of reporting, which was accuracy. His "unconfirmed source" was positive that a shooter in a school killing used an AR-15. That was what he told his editor, Chuck Dolan, and that was what the *Daily Gazette* printed. However, later they discovered that the shooter didn't use an AR-15; it was an M-16.

All the newspapers were chasing the school shooting story like hounds on a fox, but only one paper would break the news first. Russell was determined to get his story out ahead of the competition, so he didn't take the time to verify his source.

Chuck Dolan, a big bald man wearing a pinstripe suit, slammed his fist on his desk. "Readers are depending on us to deliver reliable news."

Russell, sitting in the hot seat opposite

his editor, shot up from his chair. "My source was solid."

Dolan leaned forward. "Not solid enough. Readers don't want fake news, almost true news. The problem with anonymous sources is that sometimes they get it wrong. You should have double and triple-checked the facts."

I thought I didn't have to.

"This guy was sure the shooter used an AR-15. That was good enough for me."

"What's his name?" Dolan demanded.

"He wishes to remain anonymous, sir."

Dolan sat back in his chair. "I suppose that's his right."

"We broke the story first. That should account for something."

"Being correct accounts for more."

A crowd had gathered in the newsroom outside Dolan's office and watched through a glass wall as Russell and his boss tore into each other.

By now, Dolan was on his feet and pacing the room. "You're a talented reporter, Russell. One of the best, but you know the rules."

"I get the story first," Russell said.

"That's what I do best."

"I can't argue that. You've penned a lot of great headlines, but this school shooting is one of the biggest, which amplifies the fact that you needed to get it right."

"AR-15...M-16. They're damn near the same gun. One civilian, the other military."

"That's true, which makes this so hard." He stopped pacing and landed nose-to-nose with Russell. "Give me your press card."

Russell rubbed his temples. "You're firing me?"

"You're lucky the shooter's family isn't suing us for libel."

"They can do that?"

"It's America, isn't it? Clean out your desk."

"Sir?" An icy hand tore into his ribcage and ripped out his heart. Reporting was what he knew; it was all he knew. Becoming a byline reporter was grueling. As a rookie, he'd made just enough money to pay rent on a shit apartment in the Bronx, which left him with barely enough cash to buy Ramen. He'd interview anyone with a pulse for a story. All that work, all that sacrifice, for what? For this?

Dolan would do better to rip off my arm and beat me to death with it.

He slumped back into his chair. "Twenty years, Dolan. I'm a senior reporter. You can't do this to me."

"The owners of this paper are coming down hard on me, Russell. There's nothing I can do."

Rage seared through his veins like wildfire. "You can't fire me."

"I just did. Get out before I call security and have you escorted out."

"Fine." Russell stood and clenched his fists. "But one day you'll be begging me to come back."

"Don't hold your breath."

"Damn, boss. This really sucks." He stormed out of Dolan's office with his head held high. "What's everybody looking at? Don't you have anything better to do than watch a man's life go down the toilet?"

His co-workers scattered like roaches from light.

He headed back to his desk, unsure what he would do for work now. The other major papers would find out he'd been fired and blacklist him. New York Times, Epoc,

Newsday, they'd all send him packing. "Anybody got an empty box for my junk?"

The phone on his desk rang. "What the hell?" He yanked the receiver from the cradle, hoping for a reprieve. "Carson."

"Hello, Russell. It's Frank Murphy." He was the editor at the *National Scrutinizer,* the armpit of the tabloid business. "I hear you're having a bad day."

"Bad news travels fast around here."

"And it sells papers, but good news buys opportunity. I hear you might be looking for work."

"Perhaps you haven't heard the facts."

"I don't care what happened at the *Daily Gazette*." Frank Murphy laughed. "You're a damned fine reporter and I want to sign you up."

Russell frowned. "Thanks for the offer, but no thanks. I still have a reputation—"

"I'll double your pay, throw in two weeks extra vacation, and hand you a lucrative expense account card. Now what were you saying about your reputation?"

The National Scrutinizer? Where fake news and garbage merge to make a sludge-pile they called a newspaper. I'd rather write for a high school gazette than this bozo, but still...he drives a hard-to-pass-up bargain.

Still, it would be a job, something he didn't have right now and needed, but accepting an offer from Frank Murphy was like making a deal with a call-girl. It felt sleazy and wrong.

Now, looking back on that black day in his life, it wasn't a hard choice to accept Murphy's offer, but he'd found it hard to transition from legitimate news reporting to tabloid sensationalism. A most memorable example of this hardscrabble business was the time Murphy changed the title of a story Russell had written from "Man Marries Long-Lost Love" to "Man Marries Alien."

That stung.

"Give the readers what they want," Murphy had said while puffing on his cigar. "Heavy on the titillating with a mere sprinkle of realism."

"But it's fake news," Russell had countered.

Murphy blew smoke in Russell's face. "That's the spirit. Now get back to work."

And so it was that *The Midnight Train*

Murders, his current assignment, had a smidgen of truth and a heap of sensationalism for which the *National Scrutinizer* was infamous. In a stroke of genius, Russell had thrown in the blood-lust vampire angle. Readers ate up the gore like popcorn at a movie.

Someone was murdering passengers on the Metro-North trains, and Russell had gotten close enough to the crime scenes to see the blood-splattered walls and footprints leading out to the platform. The killer had an affinity for clergymen, preachers, and nuns, the unholiest against the holiest among us. Frank Murphy had jumped on Russell's vampire-themed article and declared "Undead Strikes Again" and featured a photo of *Nosferatu, the Vampire* from the 1922 movie, under his sensationalistic headline. Pulitzer work indeed, or maybe not, but unmasking the killer could give Russell the credibility he'd lost. This article, *The Midnight Train Murders*, could catapult him back into the limelight, and hopefully, with a little luck, garner him the respect of his ex-editor at the *Daily Gazette*, Chuck Dolan.

Dolan would certainly realize he was missing his best asset, his best reporter, and he'd have no choice but to rehire him because there was nobody better at sniffing out a story. He was most likely, among all journalists, to discover the killer's identity and get the big headline. Only then could he rise from the ashes of his career like Lazarus from the grave.

This is a huge opportunity.

The Midnight Train Murders was the kind of reporting that he loved and lived for.

After a laborious and frustrating drive from the Bronx Woodlawn section, he arrived at the latest crime scene, the Crotonville Metro-North Station. Scattered gray clouds hung heavy in the night sky, and the moon looked like a skull peering down on the city. Newspapers swirled in the wind. It was only 4:00 AM.

Police floodlights lit up the platform cordoned off with yellow tape, and dust in the wind painted the scene with an eerie veil.

He showed the cop standing guard an old press badge from the *Daily Gazette*, retrieved from the back of his desk drawer, and hoped he'd let him pass under the yellow crime scene tape. He'd certainly be turned away if the cop knew he was with the *National Scrutinizer*.

A competitor's reporter leaving the train platform ducked under the yellow tape and bumped into him. "Russell, you still working for that rag?"

"At least I'm not behind on my mortgage, Marvin."

He laughed and walked away as if working for a living was some kind of joke.

Russell stooped to gain entry to the crime scene.

"Hold it right there," the cop ordered.

"Come on, man." Russell straightened. "I got a job to do."

"Tough shit. No reporters. You're all a bunch of vultures."

"What about him?" He pointed to Marvin's receding back.

"Vultures."

Standing there chastised and likened to an ugly bird, he scanned the police presence and hoped he'd see a detective he'd recognize. The yellow tape surrounding the train car and the platform jump-roped in the wind. This was the third passenger murdered on the Hudson Line Train...after midnight, no less.

I have to get in there.

He spotted Detective Oscar Miles talking to a man wearing a conductor's cap. Russell remembered several dinners with Miles, which he had paid for to get information. The detective loved to eat steak and drink wine on someone else's dime.

"Detective Miles, it's me, Russell Carson. I need a statement from you."

Miles waved him in, but as the cop raised the tape for him to duck under, some baboon captain stepped up and blocked the way.

"Oh no, you don't," the ape shouted. "Get lost."

"I need this story—"

"You write bullshit, Carson. I'm still trying to live down your last story in the *Scrutinizer*."

"That was my editor's doing. You're not a knuckle-dragger. Come on, give me a break."

"Move along or get arrested."

"I've got to talk to Detective Miles. He

knows me."

"Last warning." The gorilla crossed his arms like a prison guard on Planet of the Apes.

"My readers have a right to know what's going on."

"And you have the right to remain silent."

"All right. Fine. I'm leaving." Russell stomped away with his fists clenched.

There has to be another way to get in there.

He called Detective Miles on his cell phone. The phone went straight to voicemail. He left a message. "I'm still at the train station. Some knuckle-dragger won't let me in to see you. Call me back. I need this story."

Dammit. I'm so close.

He doubled back, skirted the barrier, and quickstepped over the southbound tracks to the other side of the platform where Miles was speaking with the coroner.

"Miles." He flashed his old press badge to the patrol officers standing guard and bent to duck under the tape.

"Where do you think you're going?" a

cop shouted.

"I need to ask the detective a couple questions."

"No reporters."

Seemed all the cops were reading from the same playbook.

The coroner stepped back into the train car.

Now's my chance. "Miles. Over here."

The detective spotted him and strode up to the tape line. "It's okay, fellas. I know this guy."

Russell joined him in no-reporters-land. "Thanks, Oscar. Whatcha got for me?"

His turkey neck sagged like pulled taffy, and his face looked as tired as his 70's brown sports jacket, but there was a keen glint in his eyes. "Where we goin' for dinner this time?"

Russell shrugged. "Depends on what you've got."

Miles led him to the taped off passenger car. "This is as close as you get."

Two white-jacketed men from the Medical Examiner's Office lugged a body bag out the open train car door. As they set the packaged carcass on a gurney, Russell peeked past them to see inside the train car. The first thing he saw, the number 1705 was scrawled in red on a compartment wall. It looked like the numbers were written in blood, the way they dripped down the wall like tears on a cheek.

It must be an ungodly mess in there. I need to get closer...get some pictures with my phone.

"Who got killed?"

"I can't say yet...next of kin...you know."

"What's it like in there, detective?"

"We're up to our elbows in blood, that's what it's like."

"Can I get a little closer?"

"Nobody is allowed in a crime scene. You should know that by now."

"You don't know my boss. Frank wants the blood and gore. If I don't get it and someone else does, my job won't be worth two nickels rubbed together."

"We all know competition is tough in your business. Anything and everything to get the scoop. So we don't let any reporters in here."

"What about Marvin Wankle? I saw him

come out earlier."

"Yup. He got this far but consider yourself lucky. When he was here, the door was closed."

"Lucky me." Hoping to get a better angle, he dropped into a catcher's stance, and his knees popped. From this painful squat, he could see bloody footprints on the floor that led out to the opposite platform.

Looks like just one killer.

"Any witnesses?" He looked up and studied Miles' face for any hint of the terror he might have heard about. Amazingly, he seemed unaffected, like this was everyday ordinary blood and gore.

"We interviewed two conductors but got nothing."

Russell groaned as he stood. *I have to talk to those conductors later.* "You gotta have something you can give me."

Miles ran a hand through his mop of black hair. "We think the same guy committed all three killings. Is that enough for you?"

"A serial killer then?"

"Not so loud." Miles glanced back and forth as if looking for loose ears. "There's something strange. We got him on camera, but his image is grainy while everything else is Hi-Def clear. And he moved like a blur. When the door opened, he seemed to dissolve in thin air."

"That's weird."

"Yeah. Spooky."

"Not that. The footprints. He clearly walked out."

"We're going to get those cameras checked."

Russell wasn't so sure that would do any good. "What about the number 1705 on the wall?"

"Not a clue."

"Was it written in blood?"

"We'd like to keep that detail quiet."

Russell threw out an idea. "Maybe 1705 is a year."

"Or the killer's apartment number."

"Come on, Oscar. You've gotta have something solid."

"I can't say any more."

"Dinner's on me, Oscar. Either steak or fast food. Your choice."

Miles licked his chops. "The Cajun Ribeye is delicious down at Smith and

Wollensky's."

"You better make it worth the money." Russell aimed his cell phone at Miles and hit *record*. "Shoot."

"All three murders happened after midnight."

"I already know that. You'll have to do better. The victims?"

"This one was a nun. She was sliced up pretty bad, and her throat had been torn out...not sure how, by tooth or claw, but just like the two priests who were killed before, it seems the killer's way of muting their screams."

Oh, this is good. Russell swallowed. "Is there any connection between the victims?"

"They're all from the same church, Saint Joseph's. Near Grand Central."

Russell's eyebrows rose. Maybe the killer was a former priest defrocked for sexual abuse. Or a religious fanatic. The Church had enough black eyes already. If the victims were singled out for what they'd said or what they might say, this could be huge. He wished he were with the *Daily Gazette* instead of the *National Scrutinizer.* This story was the reason he'd earned a degree in journalism. The *Scrutinizer's* reputation for fake news would only discredit his investigative reporting, but he'd have to take what he could get.

"The killer's going after employees of the church," Russell stated by way of summary. "Is it too early to call this the work of a serial killer?"

Two cops walked by them.

"I told you...keep your voice down." Miles glared at Russell. "We don't need any serial-killer talk. Get the public in a panic. You got me?"

He felt the sting of admonishment. "I got you, Oscar."

"How about tonight for that steak? It's early. I could have more information by then."

"See you at eight. Smith and Wollensky's. You earned it."

As Miles ducked into the blood-soaked railcar, Russell stroked his chin, as an idea was brewing in his brain. The best way to find the killer was to take the train himself. Ride after midnight and hopefully witness the unthinkable. Then he'd suggest a new headline for Frank Murphy: "Riding the Rails of Hell" by Russell Carson.

The *Scrutinizer* was a rag of a newspaper, all right, but it was his ticket back to the top of his profession.

***

Russell arrived at his apartment in the early dawn hour. His place could be the centerfold of *Better Homes and Gardens*. Clarissa, his last girlfriend, got fed up with him being away so much of the time and left him. A depressive loneliness followed him into the living room where the dark big-screen reminded him of late-night movies cuddled up with her on the couch, fireplace aglow, popcorn and beers and laughter. The spark of love had been extinguished, and no matter how hard he cleaned and scrubbed, he could not regain the shine that once was omnipresent.

All good things must come to an end.

At his desk, he fired up his laptop, and after five minutes of brainstorming, he came up with a compelling first line for his next story.

The murderous *vampire drank the blood of the Midnight Train passenger then disappeared into thin air.*

National Scrutinizer readers will love this shit.

An hour later, he emailed the finished article to Murphy.

"Fantastic work there, Russell," came the reply. *"I'll lead with it on the front page of tomorrow's online edition."*

Yeah. Bullshit sells. He stood on aching feet. "Eat your heart out Chuck Dolan." Shoulders slumped, he ambled into the kitchen and removed a bottle of Tullamore Dew from a wooden cabinet that shined white in the glow of the ceiling lights. Shot glass on the counter, he unscrewed the cap, poured two fingers, and tossed it back. A gush of warmth ran down his throat and heated his chest.

Cradling the bottle of whiskey like an only child, he shuffled back to the couch and plopped his tired ass down. He could still smell Clarissa's perfume lingering where she once sat, feet tucked up underneath her, bare knees, bare shoulders... *Damn, I miss that girl.*

Sadness put him in a *Scrutinizer* mood. Sensational headlines replaced thoughts of

Clarissa's sweet curves: *Two-Headed Man Awakes after Forty-Year Sleep, Aliens Invade the White House, Vampire Attacks Midnight Train...* He closed his eyes and welcomed his dreams like long-lost lovers.

***

That evening, after sleeping past noon, Russell stepped out of Grand Central Terminal to find New York transformed into a winter wonderland. His boots crunched on freshly fallen snow. A red pedicab rattled by with a jolly Santa Claus on-board, tossing out candy from a gray burl sack to kids standing in the gutters. Blackened ice and filthy water shot up from a tire as it rolled over a pothole. Slowly but surely the Christmas atmosphere receded into the reality of New York City. The nasty smell of rotting garbage stung his nose, which emanated from trash piles lining the sidewalk like a parade of monstrous forms, and a homeless man tripped into him in his rush to beg for loose change. "Buddy, can you spare a dollar?"

"Not even a quarter, old boy." Russell strode on toward his meeting with Detective

Miles to buy him a meal in exchange for inside information on the Midnight Train Murders. Such was the cost of doing this dirty tabloid business.

He continued down Lexington Avenue until he arrived at 49th street. A block over to 3rd Avenue put him in front of Smith and Wollensky's entrance canopy. He nodded to the doorman, who promptly ushered him inside.

In sharp contrast to the bright Christmas lights outside, the restaurant's interior was as dark as a mausoleum. He heard a Sinatra song, *Summer Wind,* playing softly in the background. Foremost, the delectable aromas of char-broiled steak, grilled fish, and caramelized onions wafted in the air invitingly.

The maitre d' in a tuxedo and tails greeted him. "Mister Carson. Nice to see you again. Your table is ready."

Russell looked past the maitre d' to see Miles at the bar, drinking a cocktail, undoubtedly on Russell's tab, as usual.

The maitre d' said, "Let me show you to your table."

Passing the bar, Russell slapped Miles

on the back. "Hey, Oscar."

Miles spilled the olive-garnished drink on his tie. "Russell." He dabbed the spill with a bar napkin. "I'm sure you don't mind buying me a drink."

"No problem."

The detective's belly rippled as he dismounted his barstool and followed his benefactor to a table draped with white linen at the back of the room. Expensive silverware shimmered under a glistening chandelier. The centerpiece: a basket of breadsticks wrapped in white napkins.

"Your waiter will be right with you." The maître d' bowed and stepped back.

Menu in hand, Russell wanted to try the grilled salmon with spicy mustard sauce, but couldn't resist the steak offerings: Filet Mignon wrapped in bacon, Ribeye and mushrooms, New York Strip on rice pilaf...oh my. However, reality set in. His steak appetite was outmatched by his burger budget expense account. He'd have to settle for a side salad and breadsticks while Miles dined like royalty.

The detective's bushy brows fluttered as he looked over the wine menu. "What say I start with a bottle of Opus One? 2011 Red will be fine."

Of course he has to pick the most expensive bottle. "You better have a stellar scoop for me, Oscar."

"The wine, Carson. Don't get cheap on me now."

Russell summoned the sommelier, sure that Frank Murphy would have a fit when he got this bill. The ass-chewing had better be worth it.

The waiter took their orders. Cajun Ribeye, blood rare for Miles, and a porterhouse on the side, rare as well.

"Side salad," Russell said reluctantly and chomped on a complimentary breadstick. "With blue cheese."

The sommelier poured a splash of red wine in a goblet for Miles. It smelled of aged French wood and money.

He took a sip and tested it as if he were a professional winetaster, which he wasn't, and then smacked his lips. "Excellent."

The sommelier poured wine for them both.

Miles swirled the wine in his glass and eyed it like he would a fine woman. "This is an odd drink, don't you think? Smash up a bunch of grapes, you got the blood of Christ or a drunkard's cheap high."

"Or a vanquished expense account." Russell took out his trusty notebook and pencil. "Okay, Oscar, what do you got for me? And it better be good."

Miles cupped the goblet in both hands and drank the ruby contents as if it were blood from a chalice, big gulps, hungry gulps, then licked his lips to get every precious drop. "Wine is born, then it lives, but it never dies."

"The scoop, Oscar. Don't get stupid on me now."

"Off the record?"

"Nothing is off the record. You know that."

"I could lose my job and pension."

"I need information, not gossip. I could give a rat's ass about your pension...nor this banquet you're about to eat on my dime. You want me to walk out and stick you with the check?"

"You wouldn't."

"Try me."

"Okay. From the grainy security video,

we believe the killer is dressed in a frock."

"Wolf in sheep's clothing?" Russell smirked. *Or a vampire in cloak and cape? I can still work that angle.*

Miles leaned forward, eyes hooded like he was about to reveal the whereabouts of the Holy Grail. "We're going in undercover, got detectives dressed as priests, riding all the late-night trains. We'll catch the bastard."

Russell wanted to be there for the takedown. "If I were to ride one of these trains, how would I know who's a cop-priest and who's the real deal?"

"Color of the day."

"What's that?"

"A system we use to ID undercover officers." He gulped more wine. "It's given out at roll call to the plain-clothes cops riding as ordinary passengers...like sky marshals on airlines. Our priests wear silver crosses on lanyards matching that day's color. When all hell breaks loose, our boys won't get shot by mistake."

Russell scribbled down that tidbit then ventured a swallow from his wine glass. It tasted like shit, but he knew that, after a few swallows, it wouldn't taste like anything. "What about the church, ah..." He flipped back through the pages...checked his notes... "St. Joseph's? Have the high-ups there said anything?"

Miles poured himself more wine. "They won't talk to us." He grabbed a breadstick and waved it like a knife. "You should talk to them. Maybe you'll have better luck." He chomped off the end of the breadstick.

"I'll give it a shot." Not that he had any confidence the clergy would speak to anyone from the *National Scrutinizer.* That truth prompted him to take a slug of wine.

The waiter rolled up a cart and set a tray on it. The sizzle of the steaks wetted Russell's pallet. Several plates were set in front of Miles. A mini-bowl of rabbit food went to Russell.

Miles attacked his Ribeye with knife and fork. Incisors bit into the meat, and gnashing molars went to work. Chew, chew, chew. Squish, squish, squish. Bloody juices dribbled down his chin. "This is good shit, Maynard."

Poking at his salad, Russell glanced at the porterhouse languishing in a pool of its own crimson au jus. He only hoped he could convince Murphy the information gleaned here was well worth the cost.

They finished dinner, and Miles ordered cheesecake for dessert. Russell ate the last breadstick, and then offered up his expense card to pay the check. The tip alone equaled a week's pay.

Standing out front now and confronted by a light snowfall, Miles toothpicked his choppers. "You need a lift?"

"I'll take the train."

"Have it your way." Miles marched to his black Crown Vic parked in the loading zone.

"What's the color of the day?" Russell shouted after him.

"You stay away from the Metro-North, ya hear. It's too dangerous."

"Did you not eat delicious cheesecake, detective?"

"Blue. Damn it. Blue." He jumped into his squad car, waved once, and then sped up Third Avenue.

Russell stuffed his hands in his coat pockets and walked toward Grand Central. The fresh air felt good on his wine-heated face. His mind swarmed with possibilities about who was murdering the clergy on the trains. Some Jesus freak gone rogue? A Bible thumper with a vendetta? A misguided soul on the road to ruin? *Why was he cutting flesh and spilling blood?* He passed Saint Joseph's Cathedral. The murdered clergy were all from this one church. Maybe an altar boy was getting his revenge for years of sexual abuse. How about the janitor? Maybe they shorted his pay. Someone in there had the scoop and he aimed to get it. He decided to call for an appointment to see the Cardinal, the Bishop...maybe even the Pope if he had to. Tomorrow.

Instead of going home to the Bronx, he bought a ticket on the midnight Hudson Line from Grand Central Terminal to destinations up north.

Hurrying onto the platform, he passed two Metro-North police and stopped where a conductor stood at the end of the train. His name pin said Willy.

Russell showed his old press pass from the *Daily Gazette*. "Willy, I got a couple of questions."

The conductor looked away. "I don't know anything."

"They're not hard questions."

A whistle sliced through the still night air.

"Are you getting on?" Willy had raised his voice. His hat set low, shading his eyes from the bright platform lights. "We're leaving." He climbed aboard.

Russell jumped on, the doors hissed shut, and the train lurched forward. Standing at the steps to the seating area, he chewed on his pencil while waiting for Willy to ask for his ticket. He seemed especially attentive to the other passengers, as if Russell's ticket was somehow tainted with an infectious disease.

Finally, Willy approached. "Ticket."

"Why won't you talk to me? You got something to hide?"

"Can't you see I'm busy?"

"Hey. We all have our crosses to bear. My boss is mine, heavy as Calvary's own, so what do you know about these murders?"

"Do you have a ticket or not?"

"Of course, I have a goddamned ticket." He handed it to the conductor. "People are dying on this train. You must've seen something."

The stoic conductor clipped the ticket and gave it back to him. "I'll tell you the same thing I told the police. I don't know anything."

"Maybe you forgot something. A shady character in seat twelve, a man roving the aisles like he'd lost a puppy. A priest that walked with a limp. You gotta tell me something."

"How's this? Thanks for riding the Midnight Express." Willy escaped into the next car. "Tickets."

Russell shook his head. *He's gotta know something*.

Undeterred, he stalked the passenger compartment aisle, dashed through the doors between cars, and hurried to the front of the train, hoping to find another conductor who'd be willing to talk. As it turned out, not a ticket-taker in sight, so he sat in a seat near the front of the car, pressed his lips together, and imagined how the murders could have happened: the sudden appearance of a cloaked or frocked figure, tall and thin, lithe and agile, swiping a blade to the throat of some unsuspecting Bible reader then, with a whisper of a whoosh, gone before the blood stopped gushing, without a final thought, a parting prayer for the poor servant of the Lord, now perished.

What's the motive?

The train car's end door opened, letting in the rumble of the rails and a conductor wearing a navy blue skirt and blazer. A vortex of swirling snow tugged at her long brown hair, which framed a tanned face sporting lips as red as her painted fingernails. Her eyes darted to the left and the right as if looking for trouble. Her name-pin read: *Renfield*.

She approached him, clicking the ticket puncher with nimble fingers. "Tickets."

He flashed his perforated ticket. "I'm a reporter."

"Good for you." She moved on down the rocking narrow corridor, but he wasn't going to let her slip away so easily, got up and chased behind her. "Aren't you afraid?"

She stopped, turned, gave him a cautious stare. Her alert blue eyes studied him closely. "What do you want?"

"Russell Carson." He offered her a handshake.

As she accepted, her blazer sleeve inched up her ivory arm, revealing an ancient Celtic cross tattooed on the inside of her right wrist. "Amanda. Amanda Renfield. What paper are you with?"

"I was senior reporter for the *Daily*, got myself canned, so my new boss at the *Scrutinizer* expects the same hound-dog reporting that had put me at the top of my profession."

"Must suck to hit dirt bottom."

"I'm still one notch above ticket-taker."

A twitch of a smile played on her lips. "You really know how to compliment a lady. What's your scoop?"

"Murders on the Midnight Train."

All play in her expression morphed to stone. "I don't know anything."

"That's what they all say. Can't you do better?"

"Your boss is going to be disappointed in you."

"Why are you so certain?"

"When there's nothing to see, there's nothing to tell." She turned and stalked through the end doors to the next train car.

He followed her. *She knows more than she's admitting.* "Amanda."

She turned to face him. "You still here?"

"What do you mean, nothing to see. Nothing to tell. Come on. Help me out."

"You shouldn't be so nosy."

"It's my job." He smiled. "That's why they pay me the big bucks."

She bit her lip, looked around, then back at him. "If I were you, I'd find a different story. Something at the zoo, the library. Somewhere safe. If you keep bothering me about the murders on this train, I'll call security and have you tossed off with as much fanfare as any other bum."

"Hey. I paid for my ticket."

"Give up the story, Russell. It'll be the death of you." She hurried off down the aisle. "Tickets."

The train shook. He followed her, passing a seated priest wearing a blue lanyard and silver cross, an undercover cop, he knew, then a couple ruffians with fedoras and frowns, sitting behind him, rail marshals, probably armed to the teeth and way too attentive on his conversation with the conductor. The possibility of a confrontation with them made him put on the brakes, and he decided to leave Amanda Renfield alone...for now.

***

The following day, having wasted his time on the Midnight Train, he phoned Saint Joseph's and made an appointment to see Father Benedict, mid afternoon. It took a lie, but he got the interview. In the meantime, after toast, coffee, and a shave, he bussed to the library at Old City College where he'd earned his degree in journalism.

The air carried a tinge of leather and a ton of silence, and though the bookroom was ancient, high wooden beams and floor to ceiling shelves, 21st Century computer monitors at study stations, center-floor, contrasted shockingly with the 19th Century decor.

Seated in front of his usual HP, he wiggled his fingers and cracked his knuckles before typing, *History New York Churches 1705* in Google's search window.

Scrolling down the list of results, he

came upon an article that told of Father John Barnes from Frankfurt, "...burned at the stake..." caught his tabloid-trained eye, so he clicked on the link.

A portrait of Father Barnes greeted him, a pencil and charcoal rendition of a square-chinned young man in white collar and frock. His hard eyes seemed to stare out from the screen, and the slant of his brows told of years of hardscrabble. The sub-caption read: *Burned at the stake for heresy, 1705.*

Russell's throat tightened as he read further. The churchgoers accused Father John Barnes of crimes against women, not of rape or molestation, but for the letting of blood with tooth and fang around or about the neck, assaults so evil the church padded the charges with heresy, which in that era was a crime paramount to murder in the first degree: the murder of Jesus and the defamation of God Himself. Father John was likened to the devil and languished in chains within the catacombs beneath the church until the day he would be executed.

Russell swallowed dryly. His genius contention the killer was a vampire riding the Midnight Train could very well be close to the truth, something the *Scrutinizer* was famed to abhor. He only needed to read between the lines to glean that assumption.

Further reading, further cemented that contention, as by methods unexplained, the condemned Father Barnes made good his threats to escape before his execution. His flight to freedom became infamous when he came upon a chap unfortunate enough to have fallen through the thin ice of a lake. Father Barnes stopped long enough to rescue him, which gave his pursuers time to catch up and again take him into custody, though this time double-chained. From there, they wasted no time setting him alight in the churchyard, a funeral pyre that burned well past dawn. Witnesses claimed the burning man vowed revenge against the church, portending a bloodbath of horrific proportions... until the flames finally silenced him.

Russell felt a chill on his nape as he stared at Father Barnes' face and imagined the skin thereon charring and melting away, leaving only bone, the skull of the vampire dead to the earth, but not in spirit.

Has truth become stranger than fiction?

But what of his vow of revenge? Did any clues to this lay within the annals of history? After more research, he discovered that, in 1805, Saint Joseph's had burned to the ground, killing three clergymen. The arsonist was never found, and in 1905, on the altar of the newly restored church, a priest was bound and stabbed to death and eviscerated, as bloody a murder as investigators had ever seen. They never found the killer, as no trace of him remained.

Now here it was another century later. Had the murderous Father Barnes moved his revenge attacks on clergy to the midnight trains? If so, for what reason? If not...some other murderer was on the loose, a copycat maybe, or Father Barnes' story was a mere myth, a red herring, a fictitious boogeyman stalking the rails, or perhaps a prelude to...

The chill on his neck dug deep into his core. He closed Google then ran an unsteady hand across his sweaty brow.

Dear God, could the Midnight Train Murders simply be a diversion, and worse horrors are yet to come?

***

An hour later, and his nerves still rattled, he hurried to Saint Joseph's Church, a stone monolith to deep pockets fed by commoners desperate for salvation. In a block of granite on the forward-facing corner of the building, *1705* had been engraved with a skilled hand and sharp tool. Russell had to stop and wonder about that, the investigative reporter he fancied himself... Was this to which the blood-message referred: 1705 the building, 1705 the year of Father Barnes' death? One in the same?

The answers lie somewhere within these stone walls.

He steeled his nerves and entered the fortress to God.

A steward, whom might have been the janitor, directed him to Father Benedict's office. "Please have a seat."

"I'll stand if you don't mind."

"The Father will be right with you."

Left alone to his own devices, Russell perused the room as any good reporter would do. Statues to statuettes, Mother

Mary mostly, had been set about the stone floor and shelved walls. Books on theology, Christianity, Catholicism, and a few Bibles, old leather-bounds mostly, made up the Father's personal library. On a massive desk set below towering stained-glass widows lay the *Daily Gazette,* its headline bold and ominous: *Cardinal Rooney to NYPD; Find Clergy Killer.*

The office door swung open. Russell jumped as Father Benedict strode in. He was a husky man in his thirties with a shock of sandy hair and dark brooding eyes. He closed the door behind him. "Sorry for the delay, Mr. Carson." With a flourish of his frock he sat at his desk. "Your generous donation is greatly appreciated. When will we see the check?"

"Soon, Father. Thanks for seeing me on brief notice."

The holy man folded his heavily sleeved arms. "Since you don't have it with you, to what do I owe the honor of your visit?"

Russell leaned forward and tapped the newspaper. "The clergy killings. I have some questions."

"Dear God...you're a cop. I told them

no interviews."

Now with notepad and pencil in hand: "I'm not a cop, but why the cold shoulder to the boys in blue? They're trying to catch a killer."

"Good God...you're a reporter?"

"Yeah, sorry to say, and the donation was a ruse, too."

Benedict leaned forward, face a scowl. "Will you stoop to nothing?"

"Absolutely nothing. I work for the competition." He indicated the *Gazette* with a poke of his pencil. "So tell me, why are you mute to the investigators?"

His shoulders slumped and he leaned back in his chair as if totally resigned to the interrogation at hand. "Comes from higher up, Mr. Carson, all the way to the Vatican, the Bishop tells me. Something about not stirring the pot, if you get my drift."

"When you stir shit, it stinks. I get it, but wherein lies the shit? This church? History? One of your good people gone bad?"

The Father's face flushed. "That's absurd. This church is squeaky clean."

"Does the name John Barnes mean

anything to you?"

"Father Barnes, yes, a disgrace."

"Maybe a black eye for the Pope?"

Benedict frowned. "That scandal is long dead and buried, as were the Father's burnt bones, in a coffin in the catacombs beneath the church three centuries ago."

A flurry of scribbles, pencil to pad, followed. "Maybe someone wants to dig it up, smear the Catholic Church with it, bloody some necks and rail cars. 1705. 1705 scrawled in blood on the walls. It's the only clue we've got. What do you make of it?"

"I wish I knew."

Russell put away the notepad and leaned on the desk with white-knuckled fists. "Look at it from my view. The church was built in 1705. What makes no sense is that very first year they cooked Father Barnes' goose. And his feathers got ruffled, vowed revenge, and with the passing of every century, destruction and death befalls this church. And nobody knows anything about it? That's the shit that really stinks around here."

"We are all hard-working, dedicated

members of this church. Our good name is important to us, and the community, but rumors of vengeance from the grave will only cause panic and doubt, so we choose to let the authorities sort it out."

"How noble...chickenshit but noble. Meanwhile your clergymen and women are being slaughtered. Bet *you* don't take the trains late at night."

"The police have warned us against doing so, but I have a sister up in Crotonville. She's in hospice, dying of cancer. I fear I'll never see her again, so I must take the train before she dies. The killer must be caught, and soon. It's not fair." The big guy's chin trembled as if he might break down and cry.

"I'm sorry, Father. I didn't mean to upset you, but we've either got some crazy shit going on, spooky wooky stuff, or someone in your employ is whacking his fellows. Who would better know than you?"

"That's enough. You'll not tarnish the name of anyone in my flock." The Father stood and pointed at the door. "Have a good day, Mr. Carson."

"Who are you protecting?"

"We have faith in God. That's all the protection we need. Now go in peace."

Russell left the Church, now convinced a rogue parishioner was more likely the killer than some phantom in the night. He needed to run some background checks, but getting their personnel records would be a tall order. The police would have a problem trying to subpoena them, as there was no probable cause. He wasn't sure how many more favors he could get from Detective Miles, but he might have to ply him with more red meat.

***

Later that night, he sat on a park bench across from the Church, holding a folded copy of the *National Scrutinizer*. A police car was parked outside the Church. Miles had said the police were using decoys to catch the killer, so he waited. Minutes later, a priest left the church, walking toward Grand Central Terminal. Russell followed, trying to stay close, but not too close as to arouse suspicion.

As the priest bought a ticket, Russell saw a silver cross with a black lanyard hanging from his neck.

Black must be the color of the day.

He followed the phony priest onto the Midnight Train, who then sat in the third car from the front. Two business types sat behind him. Russell sat five rows back, watching and waiting. The train rolled into the night, making scheduled stops for passengers to get off, some got on, but nobody looked suspicious.

The same female conductor he'd met yesterday walked in through the forward door. *Amanda, yes.* He recalled her name. She punched the phony priest's ticket, then nodded to the undercover cops but walked by them. No tickets?

Russell watched her approach him. His heart beat a little faster. She was a looker, all right, curves like Clarissa's and that same twitch at the corner of her mouth as she smiled at him. "Ticket."

He showed his press badge. "Got anything new for me?"

She pursed her luscious lips in annoyance, then: "I told you to stay away."

"Why should I?"

She bent to his ear and whispered, "It's

not safe."

Their eyes met, up close and personal. "I don't scare easily."

"The killer you're searching for will scare you out of your shoes."

"So you *have* seen him. What does he look like?"

The train shook. Amanda lurched forward, grabbed a seatback to steady herself, and as she did so, her jacket opened momentarily, exposing the blunt end of...a...a wooden stake?

That threw him for a loop. *Why would she arm herself with such a thing? Hide it under her jacket like a concealed weapon?*

"Amanda, you gotta tell me what you know."

She quickly recovered and closed up her jacket. "Just forget about it. I didn't see anything. You didn't see anything."

He decided on a more sociable approach. "Can I buy you a cup of coffee?"

"You don't give up, do you?"

The priest/cop turned toward them, obviously tuned in to everything around him. He glared at them for a moment and then turned to face the front. The business suit cops were oblivious, as one had fallen asleep, head lolling on the other's shoulder.

Russell handed Amanda the *Scrutinizer*, which featured his vampire article. "Read my front-page headline."

She looked at the paper. Her brows furrowed. "My shift ends in Crotonville. Meet me at the diner."

"I'll be there."

"You still owe me a ticket."

As she walked down the aisle behind him, he turned to watch those lovely curves sway to the rhythm of the rails.

***

There was no murder that night on the Midnight Train, and Russell met the conductor, Amanda Renfield, at the Crotonville Diner. She had changed into civilian clothes, sweater and jeans and high boots, and her long hair flowed over her shoulders in chocolate waves.

He had to catch his breath. *She's beautiful...but mysterious*.

The *Scrutinizer* rested on the table at her elbow.

The waitress poured her a fresh cup of

coffee.

He seated himself across from Amanda. "I'll have coffee, as well," he told the waitress. As she poured him a cup, he watched Amanda sip coffee with those ruby red, and very kissable, lips. Her eyes darted left and right, as if she were always on the lookout for trouble. However, this time of night, to say there were three patrons in the diner would have been a stretch.

"Thanks for meeting with me."

She tapped the newspaper, "I read your article," and slid it to center-table. "It's closer to the truth than you think."

"It is?" He sipped coffee, keeping his emotions in check, as any truth to a real vampire would be ground-shaking news.

"Good thing nobody will believe you." There was that twitch again, that hint of a smile.

"Nobody really believes what they read in the *National Scrutinizer*." He fanned at the steam rising from his cup. "That's the beauty of my article."

She stirred cream into her coffee with a spoon held in supple fingers tipped in red. "Tell me what you know so far."

"I think Saint Joseph's Church is hiding something."

She set down the spoon and picked up the cup. "What else?"

"The killer may be one of his flock."

"Why do you say that?" She sipped coffee and watched him over the cup-rim with eyes of fire and ice.

"Father Benedict got real defensive when I suggested it. He ended the interview and kicked me out."

Another sip of creamy brew, then: "Anything else?"

"I was hoping you would tell me."

"Russell..." She said it like a mother about to scold her child. "You're wasting your time."

"I've got a story to write, Amanda. That's never a waste of time, and I need this story if I ever expect to restore credibility among my peers."

Amanda leaned forward. "I'm trying to keep you alive."

"Why would I be in danger?"

"You don't want to know."

He scoffed. "I'm thirty-five miles from home in the middle of the night with a killer running loose...of course I want to know."

"You won't believe me, anyway."

"All right. I'm all about angles. You're carrying a wooden stake under your belt. Tell me something I'll believe about that."

"You saw it, huh?" She reached down and produced the weapon, set it on top of the folded tabloid, reality and fiction colliding on a cold December night. There wasn't anything normal about the stake, inch-round shank, blunt end, pointy end, a bit of curve like a tusk; it could never be a lawn or garden stake. He thought it should be a bit longer, maybe by ten feet, to avoid close-combat with a fanged bloodsucker.

"I write about a murderous vampire while, all this time, you're armed to fight one? You know what's going on, Amanda. You've got to tell me."

"Russell, there's a killer riding the rails. I'm not allowed to carry a gun or a knife on the train, but they can't stop me from using a piece of wood should I have to protect myself."

As he considered the logic in her defense, she reclaimed the stake and replaced it behind her belt. "Now if you don't mind, I'd like to finish my coffee in peace."

"Amanda, you're full of shit." He gripped his cup. "You tell me my article isn't far from the truth, but then you come up with this bull about a piece of wood. You say I'm in danger, but I'm to assume you're not?"

"I can take care of myself."

"Hell, yeah. You've got a piece of wood. You're invincible. That killer tears out his victims' throats so no one can hear them scream."

"My throat is going to be just fine. It's your neck I'm worried about."

"You like me?"

"Too much information." She yawned. "I'm tired, Russell. The southbound is due in twenty minutes. Let's go home."

"Your place or mine?" He grinned.

"Funny man, huh?" No sign of that twitch. "You may be cute, but you're not my type."

He shrugged. "A guy can hope."

***

The next night, Russell sat on the same bench across from the church, waiting for a cop to come out, dressed as a priest. If his luck was similar to last night, he'd stay close to the decoy if anything went down. Unlike last night, a snowstorm was now pummeling the coast, and even his thick coat and gloves couldn't ward off the icy gale. Through the swirling flurries, he saw a man walk out of the church, his long coat flagging in the wind and a fedora pressed low over his brow. It was Father Benedict, obviously disguised as a regular commuter.

Where is he going?

If Russell had to venture a guess, it wasn't the corner convenience store. No. His sister was probably near death and he was desperate to see her, desperate enough to risk meeting his own death on the Midnight Train to Crotonville.

He followed the priest.

Unbeknownst to the two, sitting behind the slap of wiper blades in an unmarked car, a black Crown Victoria Ford cruiser, Detective Miles watched Father Benedict hurry out of the church. Then he saw

Russell rush after the priest, two idiots stalking down a street in weather not fit for man or beast. "Shit." He set his hot Starbucks in the console cup holder, cut off the engine, killing the heater, and pushed open the car door, which let in the cold. With collar buttoned and hat brim tilted into the wind, Miles shut the car door and joined the parade of idiots trudging through the storm.

A blast of winter snow pushed Russell backward as if the hand of God were holding him back from his dangerous pursuit of a story that would rescue him from the disgrace that was the *National Scrutinizer*. He shivered and pressed on. He'd lose the priest if he didn't keep up, so he took long strides and ignored the wind's icy bite on his earlobes. After what seemed like a trek to the North Pole, he followed Father Benedict into Grand Central Terminal, through Vanderbilt Hall to a ticket machine for the Metro-North Hudson Line. The schedule showed the next train leaving at 12:20 AM, in five minutes, to Crotonville.

Yeah. Desperate times call for desperate measures and stupidity.

He had to stop the priest before he boarded the Midnight Train. "Father Benedict." The priest removed his ticket from the slot in the machine and turned around, obviously surprised to hear his name. Russell grabbed his coat sleeve. "What are you thinking? It's too dangerous to take that train."

"Now it is, you fool." Benedict stalked to the crowded platform with Russell on his heels. "Your big mouth just announced to everyone that I'm a priest," he hissed through clenched teeth. "You've just put a target on my back."

If looks could kill, Russell would have been a dead man. "You can't get on that train."

"My sister is dying. I have to see her."

"Take a cab."

"Not in this storm."

Two uniformed cops descended on the loud confrontation. One grabbed Russell's arm. The other asked Benedict, "Sir, is this man bothering you?"

A conductor shouted, "All aboard."

Passengers began boarding the train.

"No problem, officer. Now I must go."

The priest burrowed into the throng and through the open door.

The cop let go of Russell's arm. "Watch your step."

He dashed through the closing doors. Benedict had melded into the maze of people looking for seats. Russell pushed and shoved his way up the aisle. The door to the next car hissed closed, but not before Russell caught sight of Benedict's flailing coat. He pressed forward.

Behind him, a hand stopped the closing doors, and Detective Miles wedged his way through. The doors closed and the train lurched into motion. With the flash of his badge, he pushed past the conductor.

Benedict moved like a phantom from car to car toward the front of the train. Russell kept his distance, ever on the lookout for a killer to attack the desperate priest.

Having reached the foremost car, Benedict chose to sit in a row near the side door. Russell stood five rows back to the right, in a luggage offset, giving him a perfect viewpoint from which to watch the priest and anyone who might approach him.

At 12:21am, the train rumbled out of Grand Central Terminal. Within minutes, the express shot out of the tunnel and into a snowy night; the sickle-shaped moon was but a hazy blur in the clouds.

Three college students with URI on their jackets entered the train car, laughing and joking around, oblivious to any danger. They sat two rows behind the priest, near enough to be undercover cops, but Russell was sure they would be of no help if the killer slashed out at his victim. Benedict sat low in his seat, collar turned up, hat tilted down, his face shielded by the maw of an open book.

The college kids got off at the Irvington stop, leaving Russell alone in the car with the priest. It suddenly occurred to him that if the killer did strike, there was no help at hand, no one to stop the murderer, no one but him, but his job was to report the news, not become part of the story. Either he'd witness the carnage or be killed in the carnage.

A dead witness tells no tales.

The Midnight Train stopped at Ossining, and nobody got on. Wind and snow swirled into the car until the doors slid closed. The sky loomed so black over the Hudson it seemed not to exist. With a hiss and a squeal, the train jerked forward to resume its rumbling run north, into the blizzard.

The sliding end door hissed open behind him. A rattle and blast of snow preceded Detective Miles as he strode in and headed directly toward the hunched over priest.

Russell was so elated to have law enforcement on the scene, he couldn't help but yell out, "Hey, Oscar."

The detective turned with a flourish and put his finger in front of his lips. "Shhhh."

"What's up?"

The priest straightened in his seat.

Miles swiveled and stalked toward him.

Is the priest a suspect in the Midnight Train Murders? That would be a twist in the story he hadn't seen coming.

Miles reached the row where Benedict was seated. The detective loomed over him and seemed to grow taller. Expecting to witness an arrest, Russell shucked his gloves and dug his cellphone out of his coat, but before he got the camera app running, the priest brandished an ancient Celtic cross and shoved it at Miles.

This sudden, unexpected event brought with it a recollection. Russell had seen that Celtic cross before, tattooed on Amanda's wrist. As his brain struggled with the revelation, the significance, the horrifying possibility that Amanda was somehow connected to vampires, Miles' reaction to the cross trumped all those concerns.

His head expanded, elongated, and his hat fell to the aisle. His moppy black hair dropped out in clumps, revealing a bald skullcap webbed with pulsing veins. From his pale, gaunt face, fiery reptilian eyes flashed danger and death, a flickering tongue tasted the air, and a row of yellow pointy teeth set between long curving fangs shined ivory and lethal.

Russell's knees buckled. He fell back into the corner of the vibrating luggage inset; his throat burned with a sour surge of bile from a stomach beset by horrors beyond his *Scrutinizer* imagination.

Miles' vampire frame grew taller, neck and limbs elongating to grotesque proportions, and with spidery digits, he snatched the cross from the priest's hand.

The sizzle and smoke of holiness in the devil's own grasp had no affect on the monster Miles had become. He leaned toward the priest. A grating voice of pure evil resounded like rocks in a blender. "You are *ggh* the protector of my enemy."

Russell commanded his legs to run, but fear froze his feet to the rail-rattled floor. It took all his professionalism and nerve to keep his eye on the unfolding story, the cellphone now recording the macabre encounter, though he was sure the video would be shaky at best.

"Your church burned my mortal body, *ggh,* but the flames of fear and hate failed to destroy the unholy spirit within me, *ggh*."

The priest dropped to his knees, pressed his palms together in prayer. "Who are you?"

"I was Father John Barnes, *ggh*. Now I am death, *ggh*."

"Why are you killing us...for the sins of our predecessors? We are innocent...of your murder." The God-fearing priest's pleading voice stammered with a greater fear of this true demon of darkness.

"Everyone needs to know the sins of

your church, *ggh,* the hypocrisy in your words and deeds, the sham of your piety, *ggh,* the lie of your charity."

The vampire that was Miles threw the cross down the length of the train car; the sliding end-door glass exploded on impact. A swell of snow and mist poured in. By the coat lapels, Barnes lifted the priest with one hand, and as his legs dangled, he let out a scream of such horror...cut suddenly to silence as the terrible jaws of John Barnes ripped into the priest's throat with one gnash of those frightful teeth. Blood gushed from the gurgling wound and suckling mouth of the voracious bloodsucker.

Benedict emitted a final choking gag, and with it, any last vestige of the man's desperate desire to see his dying sister was lost to eternity. Amid the slurping and glugging of the feeder, the carcass hung limply in the predator's embrace.

Russell could only stare at the Midnight Train Murderer. Terrible questions invaded the horror show playing out before him. Why had Miles fed him information about the murders? Was this a setup? Had he been conned? To what end?

With a thump, Benedict's drained corpse hit the floor, and with a hiss, the vamp shifted his canted eyes to Russell, who shrunk back into the corner as far as he could go, body trembling but his cellphone running and about to record his own death.

The creature stepped toward Russell on shoes ripped apart from the inside by toes and claws.

"Stay away from me." He brandished the cellphone as if it were a weapon. "You're on video."

With one leap, Barnes was on him, face-to-face, foul breath spluttering blood. "Begs the fool who *ggh* would be king."

"What am I...doing here, Miles?" Fear had tied his tongue in knots.

"I scooped you *ggh* just enough make you think you were close to your *ggh* career-saving story."

"You told me to...stay off the train."

"I knew you would do exactly the opposite, *ggh*."

"What do you want?"

"A witness to write my story, *ggh,* sensationalize my history, make me bigger in death than in life, *ggh,* to let the world know of the church's treachery, *ggh,* and to cut off the hand of God, once and for all, *ggh*."

"I can't do that."

"You will and you can, *ggh*, not as a man but as my spawn, *ggh*." He opened wide his bloody maw of razor teeth and fangs and lunged for Russell's neck.

However, before the vampire could sink those unholy teeth into human flesh, the shattered end door hissed open, and who but Amanda Renfield stepped from the mist, the embodiment of Wonder Woman with a Van Helsing growl. "Let him go, Barnes." Her eyes were narrow slits of fury.

The vampire whirled around, teeth bared for his new victim.

Amanda quick-drew the wooden stake from her waistband and lunged at the vampire.

Before the stake made a home in his heart, the monster reared up and grabbed her wrist, instantly stilling her forward momentum. Locked in a struggle for possession of the weapon, the two slammed against the wall. The train rocked violently on its steel wheels.

Get up, Russell's mind demanded of him. *Help her*.

His heart hammered against his ribs like a caged beast. From this low vantage point in the corner, he could see the lifeless form that once was Father Benedict lying deflated to skin and bone under the flattened coat. Fear of that fate, that horrible way to die, convinced him to stay put and hope the Midnight Train would soon roll into a station where the side door would open and he could make good his escape. However, a glance out the window revealed only darkness beyond swirls of snow near the glass, and the reflection of a battle between Amanda and Barnes, a battle he feared would end with her death.

The vampire backhanded her with a neck-snapping blow. She collapsed on the floor, and the wooden stake clattered down the aisle. In three inhuman strides, Barnes landed on Russell again, teeth bared with strands of slime bridging the gap in his maw.

The train shook. The lights flickered.

Russell gripped the cellphone as he

would the ledge of a tall building. He hoped the threat of being videoed would deter the killer's murderous intent.

The vampire shoved his face forward, so close to Russell's face, he could count every blood-drenched tooth in the devil's open mouth.

Behind Barnes, Amanda stirred, shook her head, and folded her battered body into a crouch.

Death's own eyes stared directly into the cellphone lens. "You got your big story, Carson, *ggh,* and evil has won, *ggh.*" The putrid stench of death blew from the vampire's throat. "I have destroyed God *ggh*."

"W-what have you done with Oscar?"

"Oscar?" In the blink of an eye, the vampire shapeshifted into the hoggish detective. "Hey, Russell. What are you doing here?"

"You're not real."

Scowling, he lifted his hat, patted his mop of black hair. "I'm not?" He slapped his own cheek. "Of course I'm real. How's the story coming? You know, the Midnight Train Murders?"

In an immediate reversal of time and space, Oscar vanished and Barnes reformed in all his hideousness. "You see, *ggh*? All is well with Oscar. I can become anyone I want, *ggh,* human or beast. I can even become you, *ggh*." With the sound of sucking air, Russell was suddenly face-to-face with Russell. "Hi, Russell. What's shakin'?"

Ssssuuuuukkkkk.

Barnes was back. His teeth were but inches from the bulging veins of Russell's throat.

The Midnight Train rumbled into Crotonville Station, and Russell knew the doors would open within seconds.

Amanda backflipped to her feet then cartwheeled down the aisle to grab the wooden stake. She jumped to the headrail and sprang from seatback to seatback, moving like a ninja on steroids. When she landed on the creature's back, with both hands she drove the stake down between Barnes' shoulder blades.

Surprise flashed in the vampire's reptilian eyes, then under furrowed brows those eyes seethed with anger. Emitting the shriek of a banshee, he flailed back and forth, finally throwing Amanda into the seats. From Russell's point of view he could see the error of her ways. The stake merely bobbed and weaved in Barnes' back, the pointy end having barely penetrated the thick winter coat in which Miles had braved the snowstorm.

As quickly as events unfolded, Russell was sure his recollections of the ensuing battle would be foggy at best. The story of a lifetime took a backseat to survival, and seeing the vampire turn his violence toward Amanda, a surge of rage raced through him, fiery hot and bent on murder in the Nth degree. He jumped on the monster's back and grasped the wooden stake.

But Barnes was not to be denied. He flicked Russell off as a dog would a flee then continued his assault on Amanda. By now she was crawling under the seats, gaining distance to find her feet on open floor, but Barnes was right after her, ripping seats from their bolted foundations, easy as rearranging poolside lawn-chairs. The rending of steel and flooring added to the cacophony of rattling rails and screeching brakes in Crotonville Station.

Russell found himself on the floor, and to his surprise, the wooden stake was well in hand. As he rose up to deliver a fatal blow to Barnes, the inertia of the stopping train threw him off balance, and in the blink of an eye, Barnes was on him with tooth and claw. Fangs dug into Russell's neck, piercing vein and artery alike. There was no pain, only submission as the beast sucked blood, seemingly at his leisure, as time had stopped. Sound stopped. The train stopped.

Amanda appeared behind the feasting beast. Russell had only enough sentience to toss her the wooden stake. Two-handed, she thrust it into the only unprotected part of the guzzling monster, its neck, and though it was far from the devil's heart to procure a death blow, it was enough to end the vampire's glutenous feeding.

Barnes reared back with a roar and clawed at the stake protruding from the soft tissue of his neck. He finally extracted it with a yank, which threw blood spatter on the ceiling and walls.

The doors opened. Passengers on the platform backstepped in horror.

Barnes took flight, coat flailing behind him as he disappeared into the stormy night.

Amanda rushed to Russell. "My God. You're a bloody mess." She put pressure on his neck wound to stem the tide of blood flow.

He felt consciousness wink in and out. "What happened?"

"Somebody call 9-1-1," she shouted out the door. "The rest of you, take another car." How quickly she'd shifted to train-conductor mode.

He didn't know if it was shock or delirium, but the wrecked train car looked...beautiful, awash with colors he'd never noticed before. And Amanda kneeling beside him, her hand on his neck, her breast so close to his face... and the sound of her heartbeat, blood rushing through arteries, veins, and capillaries galore.

No. Not that.

He resisted the sudden urge to bite her breast, to draw blood from the nipple, to suckle red warm nourishment...

Oh, God. No.

He couldn't feed on the woman who'd

just saved his life. "Who are you?"

"I've been hunting that monster for a long time, but the bastard got away again." She removed her hand from his neck wound. "The bleeding has stopped. You're going to be all right."

"I'm thirsty..." *for blood.* He shuddered. *What have I become?*

Fighting to regain his senses, he remembered why he was on the Midnight Train in the first place: to get the big story and earn his job back at the *Gazette*, the seeds of which lay within the silicon chips of his cellphone. Without reviewing the evidence his lens had captured, he emailed the video file to himself, and then stuffed the phone into his pocket.

I solved the Midnight Train Murders... and I have the video to prove it.

On the floor in the open doorway of the idled Metro-North Express, Amanda held Russell in her arms. Crotonville Station security had pushed the looky-loos back and were in the process of cordoning off the crime scene with yellow tape. It wouldn't take long for the cops to arrive, sirens blaring and emergency lights ablaze. Russell didn't care about the cold night air rushing in. His inner being, maybe even his soul, felt warm as a puppy in Amanda's soothing embrace. Her nearness, her heartbeat, the very aroma of her skin stirred a hunger within the glow, a hunger he'd never before experienced, born of bloodlust and battle. "A-Amanda," he muttered. "I feel safe with you, but I fear you're not safe with me."

She turned to look him straight in the eye. "He bit you, and that's a problem. You have to be strong. Fight your urges. Hold on to your sanity...until I can get you some help."

"Help?" He took a labored breath. "You don't understand."

"But I do."

"In my mind's eye I see myself sinking my teeth into your lovely neck, sucking on your flesh to draw out your life's nectar to mingle with my own, to pillage that which is not mine."

"You sure know how to sweet-talk a girl." That twitch of a smile showed itself again. She leaned back against the wall, not in relief but deep in thought until sirens wailed in the distance.

Within minutes, the interrogations would begin. Questions had to be answered. Accusations had to be made. Dangerous finger-pointing. That was guaranteed. He looked at his bloody hand, wriggled the fingers that had held the wooden stake, the weapon that could have ended all this, if only he'd been a bit quicker on the defense, or perhaps more disposed to taking a life, be damned if that life was that of a 300-year-old vampire with a vendetta against God Himself. "I have to tell the cops about Detective Miles."

"You'll do no such thing."

"But there's a killer in their ranks. Look what he did to Father Benedict." He indicated the near-empty coat and boots on the floor, not six feet away.

"They won't believe it. You write fiction for the *Scrutinizer*. You have no clout. They may even think you've gone mad and lock you up in Bellevue."

"I've got the video to prove it."

"Keep that close to your chest. Trust me."

"But this is my big break—"

"Okay." She leaned forward. "Let's say

the cops arrest Miles. There's not a cell that can hold him, and what's Barnes going to do when he escapes? How many more people are going to die? You want that on your shoulders?"

"So what do you suggest we do?"

"We'll take care of Barnes...on our own terms...in our own way."

The sirens were getting louder, closer.

Russell's eyebrows rose when he thought about the vampire that nearly killed him. "That creature is out there somewhere, probably hurt and angry like a wounded animal. We failed to kill him this time. What's not to say he kills us next time?"

"He doesn't want you dead. He wants you to be just like him, you're his spawn, remember? You're going to write his story. We can use that to our advantage, and when he least expects it, we'll ram a wooden stake into his heart. That'll kill him."

"You make it sound easy."

Brakes squealed. Tires screeched. Doors slammed.

Amanda stood. "Not a word about Miles, Russell. Our lives depend on you keeping your mouth shut."

Heavy footfalls on the platform preceded a small army of first responders. Paramedics knelt to Father Benedict, lifted the coat, reeled back, aghast at the vampire's handiwork.

"This one's dead, guys."

They moved to aid Russell, opened medical cases: heart monitor, bandages, medicines, and who knew what else they'd brought to the scene.

"I'm all right," Russell protested.

A medic unwound a blood pressure cuff. "Let us decide that."

Uniformed officers pushed their way inside the bloodied and upheaved train car. The sounds of life: blood pumping, hearts beating, filled the scene and wetted Russell's appetite.

Pictures were taken, blood swatches collected, fingerprints dusted. Then low and behold, who walks in but Detective Miles. Hands on his hips and feet parted like Superman, he scanned the ripped up seating, the blood-soaked walls, and the dead carcass that was Father Benedict. "What the hell happened in here?"

Amanda approached him, but not too closely. "We tried to stop the killer."

Miles looked down at Russell and the gang of paramedics attending to him. "Carson. I told you to stay away."

Russell looked up and noticed that no such sounds of life emanated from Miles. A fresh bandage on the side of his neck didn't go unnoticed. "What happened to your neck?"

"Oh, this?" He touched the bandage. "Cut myself shaving."

Russell huffed. "Sure you did."

An officer approached Miles. "We found this." In a plastic evidence bag lay a wooden stake drenched in blood. "What do you make of it?"

Miles gave it a mere glance then looked at Amanda. "You know anything about this?"

"Never seen it before, detective."

"Russell?"

"All I know is the son-of-a-bitch bit me."

That drew a smile from Miles. "You got a good look at him, then?"

"Ugly is all I remember."

Miles scoffed then handed the evidence back to the officer. "Have it checked for DNA. Might be the killer's blood."

Have fun explaining it's your DNA, Miles.

A cacophony of gushing, surging blood and thumping heartbeats permeated his head more than ever now, and an incessant hunger gnawed at his innards. He wished it would go away before he leaped from the floor and started feasting on all those that milled about.

The medics started packing up, and one reported, "Your blood pressure is high, Mr. Carson. Pulse elevated. We need to transport you to the hospital."

Russell stood. "Forget it. I'm fine."

"Then have your doctor check you out ASAP."

"Sure." He looped his arm around Amanda and ushered her out the door and into the storm. Despite the swirling snow and biting wind blowing in from the north, he thought it strange that the cold didn't bother him. His heightened sense of smell and hearing felt misplaced from his familiar human condition. The come-hither clapping of Amanda's heart kicked his thirst into overdrive and amplified his desire for the sweet, coppery taste of her blood.

Amanda rested her cheek on his shoulder as lovers do when walking together on a summer afternoon. "Hey, are you okay?"

"Will you stop worrying?"

"You almost died back there."

"Now that you mention dying, are you serious about what you said on the train?"

She put both arms around his center and stopped him at the door to the pedestrian skybridge that would take them to the southbound platforms. Snowflakes landed on her eyelashes. "Our work has just begun. Barnes won't quit until the church is in shambles. We have to stop him."

How can anyone so pretty be so dumb? "How are we supposed to do that?"

She shrugged. "You're gonna have to trust me."

"Why?"

"I saved your ass tonight, didn't I?" That twitch was beginning to grow on him.

The southbound Metro-North screamed into the station.

"That's our ride. Let's get over there."

She stood on her tippy-toes and planted a kiss on his lips, which set him back on his heels, but only for a split second. He looped his arms around her and returned the affection. The sweet taste of her mouth, the heat of her breath, the swiftness of her heartbeat all combined to assault his determination to keep the bloodlust she stirred in check.

Doesn't she know the danger she is in?

The kiss ended with mutual smiles and a reflective train ride back to Grand Central, where they each went their own way. The storm had eased, clouds parted, and the morning sun struck Russell with a new problem. Pain. Each stream of photons blazed into his eyes like a million needle points. His head ached as if someone had stabbed his brain with a dagger. He had to get home. He had to get some rest...sleep all day, if he had to, like the vampire in his story for the *Scrutinizer*, who slept during the daylight hours and hunted priests after midnight.

Today he would sleep like the dead.

***

The next afternoon, Russell awoke more refreshed than usual. A cup of coffee down and feeling inspired beyond belief, he fired up his laptop and pounded out his next story for the *National Scrutinizer:*

THE MIDNIGHT TRAIN MURDERS

"Riding the Rails of Hell"

By Russell Carson

The killer was prolific, both in the number of victims and the ferocity of his attacks. Equally so was his uncanny ability to evade apprehension by the authorities. This prompted me, Russell Carson, to act in a manner most cops thought reckless and dangerous. I'd decided to place myself in harm's way to reveal the identity of the bloodthirsty maniac. I would ride the Midnight Train in hopes of becoming an eye-witness to the carnage, something any good newshound would do. The horrors I saw play out cannot be matched by the most violent Hollywood renditions of vampires and bloodlust.

As a form of review, let me remind my readers how the story came to my attention. Dateline: November 2005, Father Francis Hecatomb and Father Noel Davidson were murdered on a Metro-North train, southbound from Crotonville to Grand Central within an hour after midnight. Their mission of mercy, anointing the sick and dying in Blessed Mary Hospital, ended in merciless brutality. Being that their bodies were mangled and broken beyond recognition, I took the position in my reporting that the killer was an otherworldly villain from legend and lore, a vampire.

Next, the killer struck down a nun. Her name has not been released, as the cops have yet to contact her next of kin. I suggested to the detective on the case that perhaps a serial killer was among us, but he shot me down immediately. He wanted no such rumors circulating. There was no reason to give rise to panic in the city. Seems my contention that a vampire was to blame garnered no such worry, as no one would believe my sensationalized version in the *Scrutinizer*. Well, I'm here to tell you now, I was right, both about a serial killer in our midst and a vampire being responsible for the crimes.

My journey to this discovery began in front of Saint Joseph's Church near-on midnight. You see, I'd been scooped on the current undercover operations in progress, whereas a cop would disguise himself as a priest and act as bait for the killer. My plan was to follow the decoy and report on the events that transpired. To my surprise, the priest who emerged from the church was none other than Father Benedict, whom I knew was deeply concerned for his dying sister in a Crotonville hospice center. I followed him into a nightmare beyond my darkest imaginations.

The 12:20 AM northbound Hudson train roared out of Grand Central on time. Father Benedict worked his way up the train cars to the front-most coach where he chose a seat by the side door. There was an unutilized luggage inset where I took up my vantage point. I cannot say how the vampire appeared, as revealing that method could jeopardize the lives of countless citizens, so let it be said that the killer simply appeared before the priest. The vampire stood head-high to the ceiling, his cloak and cape a black smear in the aisle. It should be noted here that Father Benedict knelt before the monster, hands clasped in prayer, and he begged of the killer a reason for his murderous spree upon the holy persons of Saint Joseph's.

It was then that I learned, from his own growling throat, of the vendetta born of a centuries-old crime the church had committed against one Father John Barnes in 1705, the founding year of that institution. The elders and clergy had accused Barnes of vampirism, and in the churchyard, they burned him at the stake for heresy. The Midnight Train Murderer would not rest until the church was destroyed in its entirety.

The death of Father Benedict cannot be described in my writing, as it was as gruesome and vulgar a death imaginable. And as I watched the vampire suck the Father dry, to the likeness of a prune, leaving only skin and bones, I was sure to hold my cellphone camera up as witness to the murder. Upon release of this article, I expect the authorities to come for the collection of this video evidence, which I will not give them access to, for the truths revealed therein will be a black eye on the department.

My readers will undoubtedly wonder what happened after Father Benedict was murdered, and yes, the vampire then did turn his reptilian eyes on me. I cannot tell you the name of the woman who saved me from the bloodletting, but let it be known, she, at great risk to her own life, used a wooden stake and some ninja moves Jackie Chan would envy, to impale the fiend's neck, just as the train rattled into Crotonville Station. Only as the side door opened, did the vampire take flight into the night.

So in conclusion, a serial killer vampire is on the loose in the city, and panicked or not, the citizens herein should be afraid...be very afraid.

***

That written, Russell reviewed his article for the *National Scrutinizer*, at which time he realized he didn't recognize his own prose, the fluidity of syntax, the direct and flawless delivery of facts, and not least of all, the mystery that remained for the reader to ponder. It seemed his heightened senses had energized his fingers on the keyboard and drew from within his very soul the story of a lifetime.

Fearing Frank Murphy would edit the heart out of his masterpiece, Russell had no choice but to email it to the office and hope for the best. While waiting for a response, he prepared breakfast: toast and orange juice, but found no satisfaction in its texture and taste. He longed for the sound of thumping ventricles and the *slosh-gush* surge of human blood. His mind drifted to Amanda, the sleekness and slope of her neck, the life-sustaining pulse of red and blue vessels within. The vision caused a quake in his mouth, a pressure that emanated from marrow and bone to force to the surface a quartette of hollow fangs, top and bottom, which made eating toast a near impossibility, as these fangs were not for injecting venom but for sucking blood, preferably from Amanda's neck and veins.

As his daydream reached a crescendo of bloodlust, the laptop beeped. His fangs withdrew as he read an email from Frank Murphy.

"Pulitzer-worthy work, Russell. Your article is going up on the Scrutinizer's homepage. I expect follow-up submissions to fill in the omitted material. We'll milk these murders 'til the cows come home."

Russell typed in the URL for the website, and there it was: *Riding the Rails of Hell* in black and white. Frank, with his usual flair for over-the-top publishing, had included a 1931 photo of Bela Lugosi as Dracula, a completely opposing image to the real devil terrorizing the trains.

A text message chimed in from Chuck Dolan.

Russell, congratulations on your article. Too bad The Midnight Train Murders piece appears on the National Scrutinizer's website. Hard to believe, as the paper has no credibility. We here at the Daily Gazette would like to feature all your update articles, so I've been authorized to offer you your old job back, as we like your new style of writing. What do you say, buddy? I know we've had hurtful words between us, but we can forget what happened and keep any hard feelings in the past. Call me when you get a chance.

"Yeah, baby, now you're talking." He considered busting out the Tullamore Dew and raise a toast to his good fortune, but his cellphone rang. It was Frank Murphy. "Hey, Frank."

"Your article has gone viral, Russell. Over a million views in thirty minutes. Ten K comments, mostly positive. I say we celebrate your newfound success. Meet me at Smith and Wollensky's. Nine o'clock. My treat."

Now that was unexpected. Russell was about to pull the plug on Murphy...didn't seem right to accept a meal from him first. Then again, there was that Porterhouse...if he could contain his fangs. Their appearance would be hard to explain. "I don't know, boss."

"It's not an invitation, Carson. It's a

demand. So don't jack me around. You will be there."

"When you put it that way, fine. Prepare to fork over the dough for their Porterhouse and a bottle of Opus One."

"You got it, pal. See you then." He clicked off.

Pal? Buddy? We aren't friends. Never have been. He's the 'dog' in this 'dog eat dog' business. So he's got an angle, something up his sleeve, a rabbit in his hat. Ha. But I've got fangs. Let's see how my angle blows his mind. Bow wow.

***

Nine o'clock, right on time, Russell sat with Frank Murphy at Smith and Wollensky's, up front, in an executive booth. Amid the chatter of wealthy patrons and clinking silverware, an omnipresent thrumming of hearts and sloshing blood threatened to drive Russell into an animalistic feeding frenzy. *How do I turn this off?* To stem the building bloodlust, he focused his olfactory perceptions on the aromas wafting from the grill: charbroiled steaks, steamed vegetables, and fried onions.

Frank Murphy, a twig of a man with a bird-beak nose, sat across from him and grinned. "Damn, Russell. This is a great day for the *Scrutinizer*...thanks to your story."

"I nearly died getting it." Russell summoned the sommelier. "Opus One. Red."

"Would that be 2015 or 2009, sir?"

"Whatever's most expensive."

"That would be 2009, sir. Sixty dollars more."

"Fine. Make it two bottles. We're celebrating."

It was hard to ignore Murphy's up-ticked heartbeat. He didn't protest, so whatever his angle, it had to be a doozy.

The waiter stepped up. "Gentlemen."

Frank spoke first. "I'll take the Filet Mignon, well done, with parsley potatoes and string beans."

Russell's memory of that Porterhouse swimming in its own bloody au jus stirred a quake in his jaws, forcing him to clamp his teeth together to quell the growth of his fangs.

"And you, sir?" the waiter prodded.

"Porterhouse. Rare. And a side of Cajun Ribeye. Rare. You can keep your potatoes and veggies."

Still no protest from Murphy.

The waiter ventured, "How about a side of glazed shrimp?"

Russell had all he could do to keep his fangs from jumping out of his jawbones. "Do I look like the kind of guy who eats shrimp?"

"Sir. I wouldn't know."

"Just bring the beef."

"Right away, sir." He took a step back and bowed.

Not sure why shrimp had rubbed him wrong, Russell turned his irritation on Murphy. "What's the deal here, Frank? All this extravagance. What do you want?"

"Hey. It's a celebration. Lighten up, will ya?"

The sommelier arrived with the wine, ceremoniously opened a bottle, and poured a splash into Russell's goblet.

"Skip the formalities," he barked. "Just fill the glass."

He did. Filled both. Murphy swirled the wine. Russell took a belt as if it were lowly beer. "You're a man who always has an angle, Frank. What gives?"

He took a sip of wine. "I should ask you the same." Now he took a big gulp. "You think I don't know what's going on?"

"Care to share?"

Murphy leaned forward, tightlipped. "I pulled your sorry ass from the gutter...gave you a fucking job...gravy assignments...top pay, made you a household name after the *Daily* shit you out like the piece of crap you are, and this is how you repay me?"

Chuck Dolan must've leaked the job offer. What's his angle?

Russell's fangs tingled. "I'm going back, Frank. You can take your job and shove it."

He threw his hands up. "I knew it. Now that you're a bigshot—"

"I've always been a bigshot, just not at the *Scrutinizer*. You publish garbage."

"I published *your* garbage." Another gulp of wine. "You're not getting out without a fight."

The waiter brought their steaks.

"You got that? A fight, I tell ya."

"You mind? I'd like to eat this meal in peace." Russell dug into the Porterhouse.

Bloody juices from each cut bled from the red meat.

"Jesus," Frank said. "Did they even cook that cow?"

Russell chewed and chewed. It took all his willpower to not let loose his fangs and suck the meat dry. He thought to enjoy the plump lady at the next table for dessert.

"You look pale, Carson. You okay?"

"Never better."

Frank started sawing on his charred black filet. "Your story got us two million hits in one hour. Subscription orders are off the charts. We've had to quadruple our print runs. There's no way we're gonna let you walk."

"That's great, Frank. I appreciate everything you've done for me, but truth is, your paper sucks. Dolan wants me back, and I intend to talk to him."

"Look." He waved a forked chunk of shoe-leather. "I get it. Maybe that headline *Man Marries Alien* was a bit much, but we'd like to shift a section of the *Scrutinizer* to more mainstream reporting, maybe give the *Daily* a run for their money. With your writing style and new credibility, I believe we'll come out on top."

"Come on, Frank. No matter how much you polish a turd, it's still a turd."

"Hear me out, man." He downed the wine and treated himself to a refill. "I'm prepared to offer you a five-year contract."

"Five years? How thoughtful of you. But no thanks."

"You can't just waltz out of here and write for another paper."

"Of course I can. I'm not beholding to you."

"Not so fast, pal. I've already got the contract, and it has your signature on it, forged of course, but tough to prove."

Russell's mouth dropped open. "Bull."

"No bull." He chucked the chunk of steak into his mouth. "It's locked in a safe. Don't make me take it out."

"I'll sue you for fraud."

"I expected that much, but I'm not worried. My lawyers will tie you up in court for years. Meanwhile, we'll slap a No Competition order on you until the matter is resolved. You'll be lucky to get a copy-boy job."

"But Chuck Dolan wants me back."

Murphy scoffed. "Yeah. I talked to him, told him you're under contract for me."

"You didn't."

"He's not interested in fighting the *Scrutinizer*, so you're not going anywhere, Carson. I own you."

"You're lying. You always lie."

"Go ahead. Call my bluff...if you dare."

Russell felt such an upswell of anger in his chest that tooth and claw seemed the only way left to deal with Frank Murphy. He doubted he could get much blood from the beanpole of a man, but the satisfaction of hearing the last beat of his heart sputter out would suffice. He stood and leaned forward, stabbed a finger at Frank's face. "You don't know who you're dealing with."

The patrons hushed as their attentions turned toward Russell. He scanned their bewildered and fearful faces. *Look at them, like cattle for the slaughter, I could feed on them all, if I wanted to...and I wanted to...*

Locked eye-to-eye with Murphy, Russell fought to control his emotions, to suppress an anger as fierce as he'd ever harbored for another person. Fame and fortune was within his grasp, the reunion of talent and credibility, so near yet so far. His earlier irritation over mere shrimp seemed trivial compared to the rage he felt for the shit-trap into which he had just fallen.

"You should see a doctor, Carson. You don't look so good."

Blood. I need blood. I should rip out his throat and drink to my heart's content...but I can't. I'm not the kind of person who murders...not for sport...not for revenge...but I will kill for food. Barnes has done this to me. I'm an animal...like him. I have to get out of here before I take a life.

Amid the delirious cacophony of heartbeats, he covered his ears against the onslaught and stormed out of the restaurant. The cold night air gripped him, and he realized he'd left his coat inside. He didn't need it for warmth, but to not look like an idiot going about in shirtsleeves in the dead of winter.

Barnes had done a number on him. With one bite on the neck, the bastard had changed him, made him into a freakshow. A heightened sense of hearing seemed more a curse than an asset, as he could hear the blood-flow all around him, a constant reminder of his depraved thirst.

He gripped his collars close to his neck. The north wind howled, and the moon shined above the skyscrapers, a bright silver sickle in the sky. Cones of light cast down by streetlamps and shadows tilting this way and that, lined the route to the subway, by which Russell would find his way home. As providence would have it, or dumb luck, a man wearing an army jacket and ballcap stumbled down a stairwell in front of him.

"You must feed, ggh."

That malevolent hunger welled up from the pit of his stomach and set his feet to stalking his prey.

"Barnes, what are you doing to me?"

"Follow your instincts, my spawn, ggh."

The man hurried to the end of the platform then sat on the last seat in the corner, a wall to his right and back, a tactical position Russell surmised as he approached the man. He lifted a brown paper bag to his lips and took a sip from a bottle within. A rat scurried across the platform then disappeared into the black tunnel.

With fists clenched, Russell neared the man, so near he could hear the thump-thump of his heartbeat, steady as a metronome.

Words rushed through his brain in a gravelly voice. *"Kill him, my spawn, ggh, drink his blood. This is what you must do to survive, ggh."*

"No, it's wrong, Barnes," my saner voice said, but my bedeviled soulmate persisted with his insanity.

"The lure of blood is overwhelming, ggh, all-consuming, all-mighty, ggh. You cannot resist."

Russell told himself to turn around and leave now. Go home and get some help. *Talk to Amanda, she will know what to do.* He rubbed his temples.

"If you tell Amanda what is happening to you, ggh, she'll put a stake in your heart, just as she would do mine, ggh. Your destiny is clear, my spawn. Heed my words wisely, ggh."

Russell shuddered at the thought of Amanda thrusting a wooden stake into his chest, which would stop his dead heart in an instant, but he continued to conspire to inflict grave harm on the man, even as he enjoyed his beverage in peace.

Russell's stomach clenched as the increased hunger for blood warped his sense of reality, right and wrong, life and death, and who was predator and prey.

"Do it, my spawn, ggh. Feed."

An inbound train screeched into the station, brakes screaming, echoing off concrete and tile until it came to rest next to the platform. Train doors hissed open like the maw of some mechanical beast that vomited passengers onto the platform from whence they rushed up the staircases to ground level. The smell of all that blood, the sound of all those heartbeats... to a vampire it was a banquet in motion, a never-ending flow of sustenance.

Russell stuffed his hands into the pockets of his slacks and lowered his head.

Hurry up, people, so I can kill this guy.

How callous his thinking had become, thanks to Barnes and his incessant prodding. He looked to the stairwell and thought he too should leave this chasm before he made something terrible happen for the sole purpose of satiating his diabolic thirst.

With the last passenger out of sight, Russell looked to his prey, now ready to slaughter him, but the man was gone.

A flash of green coat entered the train and before the doors could close, Russell quickstepped to them with a speed he never thought possible and jumped aboard, barely making entrance between the closing panels.

The man had his choice of seats in the empty subway car, but chose the bench at the rear, whereby his back and flanks were covered, and he only needed to keep vigil to the front. The train lurched into motion, rocked and rattled out of the station. Outside, the blackness of the tunnel was interspersed with amber marker lights that seemed to streak by at supersonic speed. Inside, the lights flickered. The man took a pull on his concealed bottle and glared at Russell, who chose to stand in the aisle near the man. Their eyes met. A nod.

The man held up the bottle. "Care for a pull, stranger?"

"I do." Stagger-stepping along the unsteady floor, Russell came to sit with the man and take a pull on the bottle of rotgut whiskey.

"Must be mighty cold with no coat."

"Yeah, thanks." He handed the bottle back to the man, and before any defense could be raised, he grabbed the poor guy by the neck. However, he must've been distracted by the bloodlust rising in his chest, for why else would he not have seen the man extract the bottle from the bag and strike him across the face, shattering the bottle into shards of sharp glass. Whiskey flew everywhere.

As if the surprise and concussion weren't enough, those lethal shards embedded in his face, and bits of his teeth fell into his lap. Brain bruised and woozy, he crumpled to the floor, hands on his face, and screaming in pain, like his face was on fire. Seemed to him then that, of his enhanced senses, pain was also on the list, high on the list.

"Thought you could steal my coat, huh?" The man kicked him in the ribs with a booted foot. "I fought for this country." He kicked him again, even harder. "US Army Rangers, you bum. What did you ever do for this country?"

Russell curled into a fetal position, hands on the back of his head, elbows protecting his chest. "Not the coat," he managed, breathless.

"You're going to pay for that wasted whiskey." The man rifled through Russell's pockets, pulled out his wallet.

"My spawn, ggh, you must fight to feed and feed to live. Don't just lie there like a whooped dog, ggh."

The embedded shards of glass wriggled out of Russell's skin and dropped to the floor. *I'm healing.* The pain left and he shot up to his feet then grabbed back his wallet. "I don't want your coat. I want your blood."

"What the hell?" Horror screamed from his wide-open eyes as they witnessed the unthinkable.

Russell's mouth opened to reveal his lethal fangs, while long curving claws extended from his fingers and clacked in the man's direction. The sensation of shedding his old skin for new felt as natural as a snake shedding its skin, or a spider its exoskeleton, or a crab its shell, or a caterpillar's journey to become a butterfly.

As Russell's body stretched to the ceiling, the man stepped back, only to collide with the bench seat; his flanks were blocked by solid walls. He had nowhere to go.

"What are you?" the man cried.

"Your worst nightmare." He grabbed the man's neck, and pulled him into a deadly embrace. Fangs pierced flesh, dug into artery and vein; the resultant spray of blood spattered the walls and pooled at his feet, and then the suckling began. Lifeblood gushed down Russell's throat and he felt renewed.

"*Good*, ggh," Barnes' gravelly voice reverberated in his beleaguered mind. *"Drink. Drink it all, ggh*. *Feel the power. Doesn't it feel good, ggh?"*

"Yes, yes, my sire, my Master."

Energy swelled from his stomach and flowed through his body like a surge of electricity from a transformer.

The man struggled, as would any animal snared in a trap, punching and kicking, but Russell's vampire grip was too powerful and yielded not. The man's ballcap dropped to the floor. Russell sucked and gulped until the flow slowed. The heartbeat wavered. Every swallow was ecstasy, a delicacy meant only for the undead.

The man's body ceased its shuddering, and robbed of blood, it turned suddenly cold.

"That's my spawn, ggh, a chip off the old block. I'm proud of you, ggh."

Russell released him, and he hit the floor like a bag of trash.

"Thank you for your service."

The lumbering train slowed as it neared its next stop, steel wheels screeching on steel rails. Russell felt himself shrink to his normal size in a shirt now shredded to bloody rags. His fingernails retracted, which allowed him to remove the man's army jacket and slip into it with ease. He retrieved the dropped ballcap, slapped it against a hand-rail to fling off the blood, put it on then lowered the bill down to shadow his face.

When the doors opened, he lowered his head and hurried out to the platform. Passengers destined to stumble on the body rushed past him to get aboard. He'd made it halfway up the stairs to the street before he heard the first scream, one of many to follow as he disappeared into the night.

***

With the howls of terror behind him, Russell fled down a back alley between rows of tall buildings, propelled by a raw surge of power that coursed through his bones. He leapt over dumpsters and delivery trucks, a wraith in the night, silent and swift and unbeknownst to those downtrodden souls sleeping among cardboard and burlap. The old Russell Carson had slipped from his memory; he was now a new creature, powerful and unique.

Whatever Barnes had done to him, he liked the newness of his existence. The man's blood now surging through his veins was the elixir of life after death, giving him the supernatural skills he'd need to survive.

He scaled a fire escape with the ease and adeptness of a cougar climbing a tree. Within mere seconds, he crouched at the top of the building and looked out over the city lights aglow under the crescent moon in a cloudless sky. Amidst the endless drone of traffic and the far rattle of trains, the faintest of beating hearts had not escaped him.

"This city is yours now, my spawn, ggh, but to live here you must feed here, ggh. No vessel is off limits, especially that wretched woman Amanda Renfield, ggh."

"Yes, my Master."

On the streets below, police sirens echoed through the valleys of concrete and steel. The hunter had become the hunted, but rather than fear being his companion, excitement for the chase sizzled within every nerve of his body. Man against beast, the eternal battles of history: knights against dragons, sorcerers against demons, villagers against vampires, and here he sat, awaiting the ultimate battle for supremacy. The end game. Armageddon...

His cellphone chimed in a text.

Damn it. Can't you see I'm busy plotting the end of the human race?

He fished the phone from his pants pocket. It was Amanda. *Where are you? Can we meet up?*

She was not to be taken lightly, almost killed Barnes, *and could easily kill me, as well. I have to be careful with her.*

He knew it was important to remain visible in this city, to continue on as usual, keep writing, keep investigating, meld his new self with his old, just like Father John Barnes had so deftly done as Detective Oscar Miles.

He texted Amanda. *I'll call you later.*

Another text came in. *Goddamnit.* Frank Murphy.

The Midnight Train Murderer has resurfaced, this time on the Midtown Subway, and his victim was an Army vet, not a priest. Something has changed, so get your ass on the story. And don't get any funny ideas about reporting to the Daily Gazette. You still work for the National Scrutinizer. Send me a draft by tomorrow night.

"Screw you, Frank."

Russell closed the messaging app. He had other things to worry about, like his thirst for blood, for one. Its drive was so powerful, to deny it would be paramount to denying himself air. And for two, he had to get home without being spotted. He stripped out of the bloody Army jacket and ballcap, then jumped from rooftop to rooftop, skirting A/C units stilled by winter and pools covered with canvas. At one point, he had to scale the Chrysler Building, up one side and down the other, all in an effort to avoid the streets and lamplights.

Finally, at the door to his apartment building, as he fumbled with the key ring, a woman's voice called out behind him, "Russell."

It was Amanda, dressed in her Metro-North uniform. *At four in the morning?* Okay. Her shift ended in Crotonville, so she could have made the return trip on the southbound—

"Why are you out so late?"

He turned to confront her. "What are you doing here?"

"You haven't called me back." There was that twitch of a smile, but more than that, he heard her heart beating a mile a minute, and even under this dim moonlight, he could see her slim throat where the nectar of her life surged just below the surface, juicy and inviting.

Barnes would be pleased if I... No. It's not happening.

"Leave me alone." Russell unlocked the

door and swung it open. "Go home."

She grabbed his upper arm with a grip strong as any man's. "What happened to your shirt? It's ripped to shreds, and is that blood on your pants? You're a bloody mess."

"I got into a fight. You should've seen the other guy."

"Russell, you're not acting like yourself."

He yanked his arm free from her grasp. "I had a rough night."

"There's been another murder, this time on the subway."

"So I've heard." He couldn't tell her he was the murderer. She'd run a stake through his heart.

"Barnes is expanding his territory from the Metro-North to the subway system. Let me come inside. We gotta figure out how to stop him."

"I want nothing to do with him."

He's my master. My sire. He knows what I'm doing, speaks to me as a father would a son, as a devil does his spawn.

"Hasn't there been enough trouble?"

Her eyes darted left and right. "It's not

safe out here. He could be watching us right now. Please let me in."

Holding the door open, he ran a hand over his face, a physical reaction to the rush of emotions screaming through his body. He'd killed a man tonight. A kind man, willing to share a drink with him, but what had that kindness gotten him? Bloodletting in the claws of a monster, a Russell Carson monster. Nothing good could come of his bloodlust, only bad, but worse, he didn't care. Or did he? Amanda wouldn't be safe with him. He didn't want to harm her. Maybe she could help him with this problem, with his connection to Barnes and all these mixed emotions doing battle across the thin membrane of his new existence between man and beast.

"Okay. Come on."

Amanda's twitch became a full-blown smile. "Thanks." She stepped inside and he closed the door.

She followed him upstairs, leaving only the echo of their footfalls in the hallway. At his apartment door, it seemed to him that her heart was beating louder, pounding against her ribs like a sledgehammer against a wall. Why all the anxiety? Wasn't she safer inside? Or was she preparing to attack him, drive a stake through his heart, as Barnes had warned she would do?

On double-alert, he led her inside his apartment then locked the door behind them. While she paced the living room, looking around like Inspector Crusoe, he pulled the drapes closed and turned on a table lamp. His laptop screen glowed from his desk where she stopped.

"So this is where you write?"

"Yeah. The *Daily* wants me back, but Murphy's got me by the balls, or so he thinks. Want a drink?" He stepped into the kitchen. "I've got whiskey is all."

"No thanks. I'm worried about you, Russ."

"Russell." He came back with the bottle. "Do you mind if I have one?"

"Not at all." She moved closer to him. "How's that bite wound on your neck doing?"

He cupped his free hand over Barnes' handiwork. "Still stings a little," he lied. It actually didn't bother him a bit.

"Tell me something." Face-to-face now,

she looked him dead in the eye. "Have you noticed anything different about yourself, how you feel, how you sense the world around you?"

He felt a jolt in his gut. *She knows what I've become. I must kill her before she kills me. This is what she does. The mild-mannered train conductor kills vampires.*

"Russell." She took the booze bottle from him and set it on the desk then turned back to grab his wrist. "Are you okay?"

He felt the strength in her grip, powerful enough to kill a vampire. "I'm fine. Really."

Her eyebrows narrowed. "He bit you. That simple act has been known to change people, men and women alike." She examined the wound. "Are you feeling any different? I need to know."

"I'm fine. Now will you drop it?" His irritation at her was turning to anger, and that emotion had dire consequences, which were well underway, as the now familiar pressure in his jaws announced the sprouting of his fangs and the stirring of his blood-thirst. He had to get a grip on himself. If he shapeshifted into the monster on the subway, he was sure he'd kill her as a matter of instinct, his wish to let her live be damned.

"Russell, I see you're in denial, You're struggling with something terrible. It's written all over your face. I've been in this vampire business a long time. I know a fledgling when I see one. Let me help you...before it's too late." She released his wrist and reached into her blazer.

Now he grabbed her wrist. "Stop. I won't let you kill me with that wooden stake...the way you tried to kill Barnes."

She stood firm. "So, are you going to kill me first?"

"I don't want to, believe me—"

"Why not, Russell? Who am I but a challis from which to drink blood?"

"You're Amanda Renfield, the woman who saved my life, and on top of that, I've grown rather fond of you, somewhat smitten, if I may be so bold."

"And I you, Russell. A man of words and action. You know what you want and you go after it, very precious qualities to a single woman in a big, lonely city."

Feeling a bit foolish, he released her

wrist. "So you don't want to kill me?"

"You still have feelings, human emotions. You're not a lost cause. I can help you, if you let me."

"How?"

"A blood transfusion."

"What good is that?"

"It'll ease your thirst for blood. Otherwise you'll turn into a creature like Barnes forever."

A little late for that. I'm already a monster.

She pulled her phone from her blazer, no wooden stake in sight, and tapped into an app, which one he didn't know, but he did know he'd have to trust her.

Phone put away, she spread the drapes and looked out the window. "The sun's going to rise soon. You'll have to stay inside. I'll bring the transfusion needles and supplies here."

"Needles? I hate needles. There's got to be another way."

Tears formed and her chin quivered. "I've seen this happen to other people. They think they can fight the thirst for blood, but they can't. You need to trust me."

"Don't be a fool, ggh," Barnes' gravelly voice said in his mind. *"Don't believe her, ggh. You can't trust her. First chance she gets, ggh, it's a stake in the heart for you, my spawn. Escape now and find a dark hiding place before the sun rises, ggh."*

There was only a little nighttime left, and then that blazing ball of death would rise like the devil's own assassin from the Ninth Circle of Hell.

"Run, my spawn, run, ggh."

"I can't stay here." Fighting panic, he stepped to the window and lifted the sash, managed to get one foot out by the time she grabbed his arm with her beautiful vise-like fingers. "Russell, wait."

"Let me go."

"Barnes is in your head, right? He's speaking to you."

"He's scaring the hell out of me. If you don't let me go, I'll have to kill you."

"He's lying. I'm not a threat to you. I'm a threat to him. And he can't win if we work together to defeat him."

"He says you're going to kill me. Who do I believe?"

"You're the investigative reporter.

Which one of our stories makes the most sense?"

He looked down the fire escape, then back to Amanda, weighing his options. The police were out there. Detective Miles was out there. Barnes was out there. Any one of them had motive to kill him on sight. Amanda only wanted to help him, as misguided a mission as it sounded, but she was his only chance to get his normal life back, return to his reporting, his Pulitzer-worthy writing, maybe get married and have a family someday.

"Take my hand." She reached out to him. "Your life depends on staying here, trusting me. Only death awaits you out there, or worse, a brutal life as a bloodsucker, always on the run, leery of every shadow, hunted because of who you've become."

"You will live forever, ggh," Barnes taunted him. *"Top of the food chain, ggh, feared by all manner of man and beast."*

Russell didn't want that kind of life. He wanted a good woman to grow old with, not an old vampire attached to his hip like a leach with foul breath.

He took her hand. "You won't try to kill me?"

"I won't."

"How can I be sure?"

"You have my word. I don't want to lose you."

"What about Barnes? He keeps warning me—"

"He's a monster, a true lost cause."

Like me.

"Don't listen to him. The sun is coming up. You need to get inside."

If she meant to kill him, all she'd have to do is push him out on the fire escape and close the window, let the sun do her dirty work. And another fact was self evident. He didn't want to lose her either. "Okay. You win."

She pulled him inside and embraced him.

He felt her warmth, and the heartbeat he heard didn't excite his hunger, but something else inside him fluttered, a feeling he'd felt with Clarissa before that love affair died.

She sat him down on the couch and kissed him on the cheek. "Thanks for believing in me."

"My life is in your hands."

She stepped to the window now flooded with the morning sun, pulled down the sash and slid the drapes closed. "I need to get some things for the transfusion, then I'll be back. Meanwhile, get cleaned up and burn those clothes." She indicated the fireplace. "And don't let anyone in except me."

***

Two hours later, Amanda returned with tubes, IV needles, bandages...and of all things, a tennis ball. She sat beside him as he lay on the couch and laid out her supplies on the coffee table. "You look much better."

He'd showered and changed into jeans and a flannel shirt.

"Are you ready?"

"How much blood are you giving me?"

"Only enough to counteract the antibodies Barnes injected to contaminate your blood." She tapped a vein in the crook of his arm. "This might sting a little."

He wanted to pull away from the needle but didn't want to look like a woos in her eyes. Even vampires had their macho pride. The poke wasn't so bad as surgical steel tapped into his blood-flow.

After piercing her own arm, she released a clamp on the tube between them and stood to allow gravity to aid in the transfusion. Blood slid through the clear plastic tube until it was completely red. She squeezed and released the tennis ball.

Russell looked up at her in admiration and wonder, that she would do this intimate exchange for him, to give the blood of her life to a man she hardly knew, to help him regain his humanity; it was the most unselfish act he'd ever witnessed.

He'd spent most of his life searching for the greatest story, getting the scoop, unveiling the facts, and reporting the news, all without concern for the goings-on in his own backyard, without realizing his own story was an impending disaster. Clarissa saw the oneness of his purpose, felt like a backseat passenger in an out-of-control car veering toward the edge of a cliff. She'd bailed for her own good, left a void in his life to fondle his ambitions and nothing else.

His arm began to tingle a little. "Thanks

for doing this...but how do you know so much about vampires?"

She squeezed and released the tennis ball. "My family has been hunting the undead for centuries. It's a thankless job. My great, great grandfather was Van Helsing, the greatest vampire hunter of all time."

"Seems I'm in the company of greatness."

"Your articles in the Scrutinizer led me to believe Barnes would show himself on the Midnight Train, sooner or later."

"So the article I showed you was no surprise?"

"Like I told you..." she squeezed and released the tennis ball, "there was more fact than fiction in your contention that a vampire was the killer."

A burning sensation flowed up his arm and spilled into his chest. In an attempt to dissuade concern, he pressed the conversation forward. "Are there many of you...vampire hunters?"

"I'm the last of my bloodline."

He ground his molars, fighting the burn. Was there something wrong with her blood?

Had she thought to cross-type and match? "What happened to the others?"

"Killed...murdered by those monsters that spread death and misery around the world."

"I'm sorry."

"Vampires are a cancer on humanity, feeding on the fiber of mankind, and when they achieve a stronghold in an area, like Transylvania, bloodshed becomes the norm."

"Could New York City be next?"

"Not that I know of. Barnes is a one-man-show."

"And I make two." He inhaled a painful breath, as if the blood in his lungs had turned to acid. "And he expects me to tell his story and make him a legend."

"I've got other plans for that bloodsucker. How do you feel?"

"Like my blood is on fire."

"Good. That means it's working." She set down the tennis ball and re-clamped the tube then removed the needle from his arm. "Keep pressure on it while I get the bandage ready."

He watched her remove her own needle

and go about her task with the skill of a nurse. Here she was, a stone-cold killer of vampires with the gentle touch of a nightingale.

She bandaged his little needle wound. "Now, get some rest."

"When I wake up, will I be back to normal?"

She shook her head. "Not exactly. My blood will protect you from the sun, holy water, and crucifixes, but you'll still need blood for nourishment. Best of all, you won't turn into a homicidal maniac like Barnes."

He wanted to tell her that ship had sailed.

"I'm going out to buy pint bags of blood from my friend at the hospital. I'll be back in a little while."

Russell welcomed a chance to sleep; he'd been through a lot in the last few hours, and being a nocturnal creature now, it wasn't long before he drifted off.

***

Minutes later, a fluttering sound invaded Russell's sleep, then a tapping on glass, which drew him to the closed window. He parted the drapes, and outside hovered a raven, its black wings beating the air with graceful strokes, its beak pecking the glass.

Flutter, flutter, flutter. Tap, tap, tap.

With a gasp, he sat upright on the couch and scanned the room for any ominous birds. All was as he'd left it when he'd closed his eyes, yet another sound persisted.

Tha-thump, tha-thump, tha-thump.

Amanda's heartbeat, familiar now, as his own, but she was nowhere to be seen. Then:

Screech, scratch, screech.

Like nails on a chalkboard.

Screech, scratch, screech.

Coming from the closed window. He found his feet, dashed to the drapes, and threw them aside, revealing Amanda standing on the fire escape. He wasn't sure if the mist surrounding her gave him cause for alarm, or was it the white flowing nightgown she wore? Her heart was beating madly as she scratched at the glass with red-painted nails. "Russell," she cried.

"Amanda." He threw open the sash.

"What are you doing out here?"

"It's Detective Miles. He and SWAT have the place surrounded. I couldn't risk going to the door."

"Get in here before you freeze to death." He helped her step through the opening. As he embraced her and rubbed her to warm her he had to ask, "Why are you wearing this nightgown?"

"You don't like it?"

"That's not the point."

"I wanted to surprise you, is all." That damn twitch got him every time.

"Color me surprised. Where's the blood?"

"I stashed it somewhere safe." She stepped to the window where the mist was cascading in and crawling across the floor. "Damn weather came in so quickly..." she pulled down the sash, stemming the flow of mist, "but the condensation made it easy for me to sneak past the cops and climb up here."

"What are we going to do now?"

"We wait." She took his hand and led him to the bedroom where the shades were drawn.

If that hadn't gotten his heart and imagination racing enough, when she pulled back the bedsheets he thought he might go into cardiac arrest. "What are you doing?"

She slipped the nightgown over her shoulders and let it slide down her body to the floor. "Come join me."

He hadn't seen that much flesh in months, the breasts of Venus and curves built for a Ferrari, and with that shocking surprise, his body responded in a way he hadn't felt in months. He couldn't get undressed fast enough.

Now cuddled under the sheets with the woman who'd saved his life, a woman who cared enough to share her blood with him, he couldn't believe his good fortune. Her hands wandered; his hands wandered, and passions grew.

She whispered in his ear. "You trust me, don't you?"

"Yes, of course," he breathed.

"With your life?"

"With my life."

"Good." Under a tent of sheets, she rolled him on his back and straddled his abs. "Then I must do one thing for you. For us."

"And what would that be?"

She slid down his abs to his hips and made penetration, as slick a move as he'd ever experienced. He barely had time to gasp before she fell on his chest, breast to breast, and pressed her lips to the side of his neck. A tremor of heavenly delight rippled down to his toes. Her mouth opened and she licked his heated skin...then sunk her teeth into his flesh.

His instinct was to push her back, push her away, run for the hills, but ecstasy prevailed, and he welcomed her affection as a teenager would welcome a hickey. His reward was a release more powerful and intense than he'd ever known. Her response was twofold, threefold, maybe even four times that of his, and it left them both breathless in each other's arms.

"I think I love you," he whispered.

"I know you do." She licked her bloody lips. "Delicious."

His curious fingers went to his neck to feel where she'd left her mark, but she stopped his hand in mid-trek. "Don't touch it. Let it heal."

"Why did you do that?" he asked dreamily.

"We're bonded in blood, heart, body, and soul. It's a family tradition, similar to the exchanging of rings or the tying of hands, or 'you may kiss the bride.'"

"Does that mean we're married?"

"With a whole new meaning to 'til death do us part.' I don't want to lose you, Russell, *ggh*."

Barnes? "What?"

"Sorry. Got a sudden frog in my throat, that's how choked up I am."

It would be absurd to think anything different. Even Barnes couldn't shapeshift into a woman so beautiful, so perfect as Amanda.

"I have to go now, check on Detective Miles and his boys, and bring back that blood for your dinner. Will you welcome me back in?"

"Of course."

"Then, until I return..." she kissed him on the lips, "remember me in your dreams."

He closed his eyes, heard the window sash slide up and down, and the mist seep in with a hiss.

***

It was late afternoon when Russell awoke. He thought he should feel invigorated, but instead, his head pounded and his mouth tasted dry as talc. What he wouldn't give for a pint of blood right now.

He got up, and still naked, stagger-stepped to the front room window to check on the fog. The instant he pulled back the drapes, the blazing sun shined in, bright as a spotlight, hot as a laser. He crossed his arms over his eyes and heard the little hairs on his chest sizzle as they withered. He jumped back, thinking he'd never do that again. Amanda's blood hadn't protected him from the sun, as she had claimed.

The thought of Amanda brought back their lovemaking adventure and the mark she'd left on his neck. He reached up and felt for it, an arc of teeth marks, he expected but felt nothing. Had it really happened? Was it a dream? He had to know, and to know meant he had to see the love bite, so he stalked toward the bathroom mirror to solve the mystery.

Halfway there, someone pounded on

the door. He froze. Was it Detective Miles and his SWAT buddies finally making their move to arrest him? Amanda had said they'd surrounded the building. Would they bash in his door and make entry, guns blazing to take down the Subway Killer?

"Russell!" Amanda yelled. "Let me in."

"Amanda, thank God." He threw open the door, but instead of rushing inside, she just stood there with her mouth agape.

"What?"

"You're naked." She looked mortified.

"So?"

"Put some clothes on."

"Stop acting so shocked and get in here."

She sidestepped by him, carrying a cooler, but kept her eyes on his face.

He looked her up and down, stripping her with his eyes, and remembering the naked woman within those tight jeans and winter coat. "Ah. I see you brought beers."

She set down the cooler. "Your blood... For dinner. Don't you think you should get dressed?"

"Why?"

"Russell, you're making me extremely

uncomfortable."

Women. Who can figure them out?

He took leave to the bedroom to dress. "So the cops are gone, huh?"

"What cops?"

"The ones you saw this morning."

"I didn't see any cops."

"They had the place surrounded." He walked out wearing only his jeans.

Her eyes darted to his chest. "You're burned. What happened?"

"I opened the window to check on the fog—"

"What fog?"

"This morning's fog."

"It's been sunny all day. What's the matter with you?"

"You were on the fire escape, in the fog, wearing a white nightgown."

"Jesus, Russell. You were dreaming."

"I was?" He touched his neck. Still nothing to feel there.

She opened the cooler and extracted a pint bag of blood. "Drink this, you'll feel better."

"You seemed so real." He looked at the packaged blood, the red cross on the label, felt that pressure in his jaws. "We made love."

"Really?"

"It was your idea."

"Well...was I any good?"

He licked his upper lip. "All the way down to the love bite, family tradition, you told me, right here on my neck." He pointed to the spot that would always mean something special, dream or no dream.

Smiling, she inspected his neck, then suddenly stepped back, her eyes welling with horror.

"What is it?"

"It's...there." She could barely speak. "The mark, but I didn't put it there." She grabbed his arm. "What did you do?"

"Me? You. Us."

"No. It didn't happen."

Panic painted her face in shades of red. "Barnes. He got to you. He undid everything we did last night. That's why the sun burned you."

"You're saying Barnes banged me like I was his bitch?"

"You're a fast learner."

He felt a little sick in his stomach, but

worse, he hadn't really seen Amanda naked but just an illusion, and only now did he realize the mistake he'd made answering the door in the nude. If he could shrivel up and die, he would, from embarrassment.

"I'm so sorry, Amanda."

"I'm not." That twitch again. "You're kinda cute in the buff."

Heavy footfalls from down the hall destroyed that compliment. And it sounded like an army pounding up the stairs, and a cacophony of heartbeats clapping louder and louder. A radio in the distance squelched.

"The cops are coming." She grabbed the bag of blood from him, stashed it in the cooler and slammed the lid. "We've got to get out of here."

A fist pounded on the door. "Mr. Carson, this is the police. Open up."

"That's Miles." Icy fear gripped him. *It's a setup.*

"We want to talk to your girlfriend."

"Is she a suspect?" Russell shouted through the door.

"Don't play twenty questions with me, Carson. Open up or we'll break it down."

Amanda joined him at the door. "He wants me out of the way," she said under her breath. "I'm a threat to him, damn near killed him once. He'll lock me up and throw away the key."

"They must've followed you here."

"Get dressed. I'll hold them off."

He ran to the bedroom, pulled on his flannel shirt and stabbed his feet into his shoes. Sunglasses on the dresser. A long coat from the closet, ballcap from the top shelf.

Ready. Go.

Back in the front room: "You got a warrant, copper?"

"Lady," Miles shouted. "You're going downtown, dead or alive, your choice."

Amanda grabbed the cooler and sprinted to the window. "Hang on. This is going to hurt." She opened the drapes and let in the sunshine.

The light was so bright it came with the sound of an onrushing locomotive. He jumped out the window and scrambled down the fire escape, Amanda right behind him. He heard wood splintering; the door had been breached. A second later, gunshots rang out above them. Bullets pinged off ladder rungs and thumped into the cooler, which Amanda held over her head for a shield. It started spewing streams of blood from punctured bags. She got an ungodly soaking if ever there was one.

She screamed and dropped the cooler. It banged and pirouetted down the last rungs of the ladder before it broke open on the pavement and scattered its gory contents in every direction. "Shit. There goes your dinner."

Russell hit the ground on all fours, an animal pursued by hounds, and he grabbed Amanda and covered her with his body as he barreled into a row of bushes where he scrabbled low for the most shadow he could find. Even with the shades and hat, the sunlight managed to burn and sizzle his exposed flesh at will.

"Where's your car?"

Amanda wiped blood from her face. "Down the block on Webster."

Squad cars skidded up to the curb, sirens wailing and lights flashing. Miles wasn't fooling around. He wanted the vampire hunter dead.

"Go. I'll follow and cover our rear."

They cut through an alley between two buildings that blocked out the sun, dodging heaps of black trash bags and rows of garbage cans. An unshaven man wearing a wife-beater and dirty apron stood in the back doorway to an eatery. "What the hell you two doing back here?"

Russell's fangs throbbed in his jaw. *I could rip your throat out right now, but I have to keep moving.*

"Hey. Why is she all bloody? What did you do to her, man?"

"Amanda, keep going."

"I'm callin' the cops," the man yelled.

You're lucky it's not after midnight, you fool.

Russell leered at him, his fangs extending with lethal fury.

"Let it go," Amanda shouted over her shoulder. "Come on."

I need to control my anger. He looked back to the woman running in front of him, dogging potholes and breathing hard. *I need to protect her.* His fangs receded, and he caught up to her with inhuman strides.

Seconds later they broke out of the alley and onto the street where traffic teamed and pedestrians streamed, all unaware of the vampire in their midst. Across the street at Woodlawn Station, a Metro-North train screeched to a halt alongside the platform. A police car with lights lit and siren whooping raced toward them.

"Get down," Amanda said.

They stooped behind a parked car until the squad car careened left and roared up the hill.

"All clear." Amanda led him down the block to her car, a white BMW X7 SUV, a soccer mom's ride if ever there was one. It unlocked with a beep, and she opened the backseat door. Russell dove in and laid low on the leather seat. She shut the door then nonchalantly strode around to the driver's door and got in.

The engine started, and she pulled away from the curb, cautious as any soccer mom.

Russell sat up, looked out the rear window, and took inventory: cars, trucks, a bus, and no cops. "We made it." He turned to face the front. "Where are we going?"

"My place to hide out until nightfall."

"Then what?"

"I'm making this up as I go, Russell. Give me time to think."

"Okay, but I have to feed again sometime."

She took a hard right. "Damn Barnes to hell. I gave you my blood and he took it away... Wait. You said *again...feed again.* What does that mean?"

"Ah, well..."

She ventured a quick glance back at him. "You didn't get into a fight last night. You fed. That's why you were all bloody. Oh my god. On the subway. You killed that man."

"Barnes made me do it."

"He was with you?" She stopped at a traffic light...well...ten cars back.

"No. He was in my head talking shit, prodding me on, and I couldn't help myself."

"Why didn't you tell me?"

"Ahhhh, let's see," he said calmly, "I'm a vampire and you're a vampire hunter. Gee, I don't know..." then yelled, "Maybe I didn't want you to run a stake through my heart."

She made a left to enter the Queens Midtown Tunnel, eastbound under the East River. "So Barnes, I mean Miles, knows you're the Subway Killer. He's got every cop in town gunning for you."

Russell leaned forward. "I'm like a son to him, his spawn. He's proud of me for feeding on that guy, but you, you're the enemy. He wants me to feed on you. The cops aren't after me, they're gunning for you, shoot on sight by the looks of it, I'd say." As evidence, he raked his fingers through her blood-soaked hair. "None of them said 'stop or I'll shoot.'"

"That was my favorite cooler, too."

Only moments after the tunnel broke out onto Interstate 495, a siren twirped behind them. Russell spun to look out the back window. Unmarked car. Black Crown Vic, blue lights flashing along the top of the windshield...and on the grill. His super-sensitive vision saw an incredible sight behind the wheel. Detective Oscar Miles...and he looked pissed.

"Son of a bitch," Amanda shouted to

the rearview mirror.

"Where did he come from?" If panic was a tombstone, his voice would have been a cemetery.

"We're not sticking around to find out." Amanda gunned the engine and careened between two cars, forcing them out of their lanes.

The siren let out a warbling wail, loud and demanding.

The BMW whined like a finely oiled sewing machine and jettisoned to a hundred and ten, but the hopped-up Ford cruiser would not be denied. Miles stayed on her tail, tapped out a warning on her bumper, determined to crash the BMW and kill its driver. She took the 278 ramp at a blistering 140, tires screaming in the curve, dirt and dust billowing as she tore up the shoulder, passing traffic, regular folks who didn't have a clue to the life and death race in progress.

Russell didn't know whether to watch Miles behind them or the terrors coming up: traffic, traffic, and oh hell, construction cones. "How does he keep finding us?"

"He's connected to you, Russell. He

always knows where you are. Like on the subway, right?"

"And on the top of a tall building—"

"Where?" She jerked the BMW to the middle lane.

"Long story. He told me this was my city now."

"Christ."

"We have to split up, Amanda. It's the only way you'll be safe."

"Don't shut me out."

"I don't want to endanger you anymore."

She slammed a hand on the steering wheel. "No way. We're in this together."

The BMW swerved, nicked a car in the next lane, and damn near hit a semi before she regained control.

"Watch it. You're gonna get us killed."

"You wanta drive?" Amanda veered left across three lanes, tires screeching as she weaved around cars, then shot back to the right, but that damn Miles was glued to her bumper.

Flying over the Kosciuszko suspension bridge, she hugged the right lane. "What's he doing?"

In this NASCAR race from hell, Russell recognized the move. "He's drafting you."

"Drafting?"

Sure enough, the Crown Vic used the BMW's wake to reduce its own drag then swerved left to slingshot up alongside. Amanda glanced left to look at Miles. Miles glanced right, showed teeth, then yanked the steering wheel right, ramming the BMW. Metal crunched. Tires smoked. The heavy German car pushed back. The Ford yielded then came at them again with bone-jarring force.

"Look out," Russell screamed.

A lane divider lay dead ahead. Right lane exit. At 100 miles per hour, disaster was only seconds away.

She gritted her teeth and slammed the Crown Vic at full throttle, knocking it out of her lane with but a split second to spare as a crash retainer wall suddenly separated the vehicular combatants. The battered Crown Vic had nowhere to go but straight. The BMW faced an entirely new problem. It was racing toward a solid line of stopped traffic. The only way out, a sharp righthand curve, but at this speed, a guaranteed rollover.

"Hold on." Amanda slammed on the brakes, throwing Russell into the front seat where he faceplanted the glovebox. The tires screamed like a horde of demons, and the antilock system shook the BMW hard enough to throw rivets and welds, but she made the turn on two wheels, blew a stop sign, and coasted down a street lined with graffiti-marred warehouse walls and old tenements.

"Are you all right?" She offered Russell a hand up.

He managed to get himself bottom end down in the passenger seat. "Good thing I'm a vampire or that might have hurt."

"Bought us a little time, is all. He'll be back."

The sunlight through the windshield was much more intense than in the back seat. Russell resituated his sunglasses and ballcap then looked around. "Where are we?"

"About a mile from my place. Thanks to Barnes, we have to take the scenic route."

"If we make it." His sensitive hearing picked up the distant screams of distant sirens. "It's only a matter of time before

Barnes zeroes in on me again."

I have to put distance between her and me before it's too late.

At a stop sign, he pulled on the door handle, but the door wouldn't open, it wouldn't unlock. He looked at her quizzically. "What the hell's wrong with this door?"

"Child lock." That twitch again. "You're not going anywhere without me."

"Don't you get it? He wants you dead. Let me deal with him."

"I'm the vampire hunter. You need me to help you deal with him."

Another stop sign. The distant sirens weren't so distant anymore. "I don't want you getting killed."

"We'll have to chance it." She turned down a narrow one-way street of apartments and rowhouses, squeezed between parked cars into a driveway between buildings and opened a garage door with a button on the rearview mirror. After driving in, she closed the door behind her and released the child locks.

They got out and surveyed the damaged BMW. Dented fender, dented doors, black paint scrapes, in general, a damn mess Miles had made of her ride.

Amanda groaned. "My insurance company is going to cancel me again."

A door led to a staircase that led to her home, a quaint two-level with modest windows and simple furnishings. She pulled the drapes. "Make yourself at home while I clean up."

He removed his sunglasses and cap then had a look around. Pictures hung above the couch: two of lighthouses, rocks and crashing foamy swells, a larger one of waves rolling to shore and seabirds gliding low, all flanked by two large crucifixes, for protection, he assumed. It seemed she loved the sea, which told him she had a wandering spirit, an explorer's soul, or perhaps her vampire hunting job kept her on the move from shore to shore and never rooted in one plot of solid ground.

Sirens persisted in the distance.

He heard water running, the shower, and he imagined her naked skin under a sheen of soapy suds, her hands kneading shampoo into her long brown hair. It wasn't hard to wonder if Barnes' interpretation of her nakedness was at all close to reality.

The kitchen was a lot smaller than his, and she'd chosen a décor of roosters and hens, eggs and haystacks. Colorful. Cheery. Everything was in place, clean as if she'd never used the stove or the table or even walked the floor. The window above the sink had only a lace tier, so he decided not to explore any further.

Back in the living room, he sat on the couch and perused a Cosmopolitan he'd lifted from the end table. He'd half expected to find gun catalogues and NRA magazines, but it seemed Amanda was interested in fashion and etiquette over guns and glory.

A hair dryer whined in the bathroom. She probably had a towel wrapped around her shower-heated body, her legs smoothly shaven, toenails painted. As much as he wanted to get up, go in there, see how well his imagination served him, he decided to stay put. She might not kill him for being a vampire, but she'd surely kill him for being a snoop.

When the hair dryer fell silent, he set the Cosmo aside. "Nice place you got here."

"It's home, though I spend very little

time here." Her voice had moved down the hallway, probably in her bedroom where she was getting dressed, panties first, bra next. What outfit would she wear to hunt and kill Barnes?

"I'm not home much either...which makes me wonder about Barnes. Where does he live? How much time does he spend there?"

"Days, most likely."

"He doesn't come out but once a century to terrorize the church, yet somehow as Detective Miles, sunlight doesn't bother him."

"Miles is an avatar, a puppet. Barnes pulls his strings. Might be a decent guy if not for the monkey on his back."

"So it's conceivable that Barnes is in one place and Miles is in another, not necessarily one in the same."

"Yes. It's possible Barnes is sleeping all day while Miles does his dirty work, but after dark, anything goes. Barnes had shapeshifted into Miles the night he killed Father Benedict. The real Miles was probably at home, banging his wife."

Sirens seemed to be getting closer. A

sense of urgency moved in like a graveyard fog.

"So where would Barnes be holed up?"

She walked into the living room as stunning and fresh as a Sunday morning bride. High black boots, tight black jeans, low-cut black pullover, black leather vest, and her long hair flowed over her shoulders, perfect as any model in that Cosmopolitan.

Black must be the color of the day.

She set a gym bag on the couch. "My guess is he lives close to his coffin."

"His coffin?" That got Russell to his feet. "Father Benedict told me where it is. In the catacombs under the church. We've got to get over there."

She grabbed his arm and pulled him close. "I'm not so sure."

Not only did she smell good after her shower, but her thump-thumping heart sounded good, good enough to—

"The catacombs are all but gone, Russell. Under-dug by subway tunnels, most of them collapsed in the early 1900s." She let go of his arm. "My money is on his coffin being there in those old tunnels no longer in use. He'd have easy access to the trains, the subway, the entire city, for that matter."

"Amanda, you're not only beautiful, you're smart."

"Now that's more like what a girl wants to hear." The twitch became a sly smile.

Her come-hither tone stirred an impulse within him, ancient and feral, and the thought of ripping her clothes off seemed an appropriate response. However, he had a vampire to kill.

"Let's go." She picked up her gym bag.

"What's in it?"

"Wooden stakes, holy water, garlic cloves, rope, sharp blades, flares, flashlights, oh, and a hammer and nails. My murder kit."

Enough said, but... He took the bag from her. "You're not going with me. It's too dangerous."

"Okay." She sat on the couch and crossed her arms. "Where are you going?"

"The catacombs."

"They don't exist anymore. Have you not been listening?"

"The subway, then. The old tunnels."

"Okay. Where are they, and better yet,

how do you propose to get in?"

His mouth opened; his tongue flopped, but nothing came out. He had to concede. "I don't know. You tell me."

She smiled. "Not only handsome, but smart." A quick slip of two fingers into her pullover produced a pass key card from her bra. "Gotta have one of these." She stood and pulled her cellphone out of her pants pocket. "Subway map, 1904. There's an app for that." She put both items back where she found them. "You need me, Russell. I want that bat-bastard dead, just as much as you do. Get my drift now?"

The sirens had to be only a few blocks away.

"All right. You can come with me, but if you get killed, I'll never speak to you again."

"Deal." A horn honked outside. "That's our ride."

"You called a cab?"

"Safety in numbers, right?"

There had to be a million cabs in New York City...and a million sirens judging from the sounds closing in.

She took her murder kit back. "Better

get geared up for the sun." And out the door she ran.

Amanda was already in the cab when Russell got there. He slouched in the seat and kept his hat low on his face.

"Where to, folks?" the driver asked.

"Nassau Avenue Station."

"What's wrong with your friend?"

"He's shy. Can we go now?"

The meter started counting up.

By the time the cab reached the end of the block, two police cars careened around the corner in full-on *code three*. Before Amanda's house slipped from view, four cop cars skidded helter-skelter in the street out front.

"Got some excitement goin' on back there," the cabbie said. "Another ten seconds and we'd a been caught up in the middle of it."

Russell swallowed hard. "Timing is everything."

***

As the subway train traveled toward Grand Central Terminal, Russell leaned forward with his elbows on his knees and hands covering his ears.

Every heartbeat of every passenger galloped like a runaway herd of wild horses. How could anyone have access to such a cacophony of delicious sounds and not go mad? His own heart pounded along with them, anticipation its driver, want and need its passengers. This need to feed his insatiable hunger for blood threatened to tear sanity from his clenched teeth, release his gluttonous fangs, and deliver carnage on a biblical scale.

He shivered.

"Are you all right?" Amanda asked.

"Barnes really fucked me up."

"We'll get him for that. Wait and see."

A familiar clicking noise approached. "Tickets... Oh, hey. It's you, Amanda." The conductor's eyes brightened.

"Hi, Willy." Amanda flashed him her MTA badge.

"How about him?" He indicated Russell.

"He's my prisoner. Taking him downtown for subway jumping."

"He doesn't look well. You okay there, buddy?"

Russell pressed his hands harder against his ears, hoping he would go deaf rather than endure another beckoning heartbeat.

Amanda laughed. "I had to beat him up some, but he'll be fine."

Willy nodded. "Did you hear? The Midnight Train Murderer is stalking the subway now. Cops are on the lookout."

"I'll keep my eyes open."

Russell felt Willy's closeness, his probing eyes and laborious heart throbs. It would only take one minute of terror and bloodshed to get hours of relief from that awful gnaw in the pit of his gut, but he dared not attack Amanda's friend.

"Be careful out there, Amanda."

"I will, and you too, Willy."

The conductor moved down the aisle. "Tickets."

Amanda leaned close to Russell's ear and whispered, "Are you okay?"

Russell shook his head. "I need blood."

"Just stay calm. We're almost there."

***

With his head held low, Russell followed Amanda past the four-faced clock in Grand Central Terminal. Heartbeats clamored, driving his mind toward sheer lunacy. The hunger for gushing, spewing, coagulating blood bore a thirst befitting the devil's own craw.

Omnipresent. Overwhelming.

Like an alien fungus had set upon his body, destroying his humanity and choking off his air. His legs felt stiff as stilts, each step a burden, a journey of torture.

To add to his misery, sunlight glowed through the towering arched windows set around the cavernous terminal, and the high windows that circumvented the ceiling. At odd and unpredictable times, solar death rays would strike his exposed skin, causing it to sizzle and smoke. He had to tolerate this agony or risk drawing attention to their flight toward the underground platforms.

She led him down a long sloping ramp with arched ceilings to another ramp that took them to the lowest level of the terminal where trains awaited scurrying passengers. Down a dimmer hallway she came to a closed door with a sign that read:

MAINTENANCE: AUTHORIZED
PERSONNEL ONLY.

A swipe of her MTA badge against a reader resulted in a resounding click from the locking mechanism and allowed her to open the door. Beyond that door lay a labyrinth of blessed tunnels unincumbered by sunlight.

Russell exhaled with relief. Following Amanda down this maintenance tunnel, he put distance between the scorching sun and the crowds of human blood chalices that had tortured him. Five more seconds and he might have gone berserk, feeding from neck-to-neck until every commuter lay dead and drained. Now he welcomed the peaceful gloom like an old friend.

She led him down a metal stairwell that ended at the old platform of a subway line no longer in use. Three tunnels forked off from this hub, one boarded up like an old mineshaft; the other two were black maws that led to the bowels of New York City's underground. Stagnant air smelled of urine and beer, and paint-chipped, water-stained walls built in the late 1800s displayed eroded graffiti and sepia advertisements for soaps and tonics. Naked light bulbs hung from the ceiling; some flickered and others emitted a brown and dirty glow. His acute hearing detected the drip-drip of water and the occasional squeak of a rat.

Standing on rotted ties between rusted rails, Amanda took out her phone and studied the subway app. Present day buildings were superimposed above a network of tunnels, green for 'in use' - red for 'retired'. She'd pinned Saint Joseph's church and turned the phone to orient their position in relation to their destination.

"We take the righthand tunnel." She looked at her watch. "We don't have much time. Once it gets dark, I doubt we'll find him down here."

"I wonder where he'll strike next."

"Nowhere, if I get my way." Amanda reached inside her gym bag and removed two flashlights. "Here. It looks pitch black in there."

Small beams of light joggled left and right and up and down as they cut into the expanding darkness of the righthand tunnel. Sections of the old iron rails were either missing or set askew, and the splintered ties were an ever-present trip hazard. In some places along the way, ghostly sounds of life above ground filtered in, echoing rumbles of faraway traffic and trains, mostly, and sometimes haunting laughter from a theater or strains of piano notes from a speakeasy. Even his keen vampire hearing couldn't determine if these sounds were contemporary or faint echoes from a bygone era.

"Stop." The cellphone glow illuminated Amanda's face, such beauty in this depressing place. "There's a turn on the right coming up."

The farther they traveled into this subterranean maze, the cooler and wetter the air became. He hadn't seen a splay of graffiti or an empty beer can for a good hundred yards. Not even vagrants and misfits dared venture so deep.

The same could not be said for the rats. That right turn took them straight into a nest of the varmints, and they were not happy about the intrusion. An echoing chitter rose in the dark, foul air. Everywhere the flashlights pointed revealed the glow of beady eyes, sharp buck teeth, furry fat bodies, and needle-like claws. Some rats ran from the light. Others attacked.

Being a vampire, Russell wasn't afraid, just thirsty, but Amanda's human instincts and fears came out as screams of terror. She ran around in circles, kicking rats, stomping rats, cursing rats. Some clung to her boots while others climbed up her jeans.

The sudden chaos prompted the fangs in Russell's jaws to extend. He plucked a rat off Amanda's shoulder and bit into it like a juicy tropical fruit. Its death screech was short and sweet. One after another, drained rats hit the floor. Each squish and gish infused in him a jolt of energy. He quickly felt revitalized, reborn.

It didn't take long for the rats to get the message: death had come to their underground abode. The tone of their chittering changed, and the horde thinned as the rats made their escape into the blackness.

Amanda finally got her wits about her, shined her flashlight on Russell, witnessed blood leaking from his jaws, dripping from his teeth. "Russell," she shrieked.

He stopped feasting. "What?" A rat wriggled in his grasp.

"That's disgusting."

He dropped the rat like a kid caught with his hand in the cookie jar. "I was thirsty."

She shined her light down the tunnel before them, not a rat in sight. "We have to keep moving."

Before long, the tunnel spit them out into a huge cavern. His vampire vision scanned jagged granite walls and a boulder-strewn floor. Flashlight beams traced mangled rails to an old and dented subway car with riveted panels and a double-sliding door, probably abandoned during the Roaring Twenties. On the far wall and higher up, two tunnel openings peered down like the weeping eyes of an old man. All the rubble indicated to Russell a massive collapse had destroyed this part of the old subway system.

She checked her app. "The church is right above us."

"The remains of the catacombs must be around here somewhere."

An icy breeze howled through the tunnels. She shivered. "Odd how the temperature in here suddenly dropped."

As they struggled over broken stone that began to crumble under foot, it became more and more apparent that a substance coated the granite.

Amanda shined her light on it, plied some granules with her hands, and finally announced, "Bat shit."

Flashlights turned upward and revealed a colony of bats hanging from the jagged ceiling. They became suddenly agitated, started clicking. Their wings started flapping in unison, as if one giant monster had awakened.

Click. Click. Click.

"There must be hundreds living down here."

"It's not a coincidence." Amanda knelt to her gym bag and removed a machete and a scythe. "Everything serves Barnes." She tossed the machete to Russell. "Kill 'em. Don't eat 'em."

The bats launched from the ceiling in a swarm of black fury, their flapping wings and clicking throats a portent of death. He had the advantage of vampire night vision and was able to whack the buggers in midflight.

Amanda was not so equipped and suffered several nips and scratches. "There's too many." She swung blindly, scoring only by chance.

Russell sliced at her attackers with his blade, which was nearly as useless as fighting off a swarm of bees with a butter knife, hit and miss, but mostly miss.

Then, as fast as the bats attacked, they retreated up to the two high tunnels and flew into the darkness within.

"What happened?" Russell spun around, blade at the ready. "Where did they go?"

Amanda brushed herself off. "Dusk. The sun must be setting. It's that time when they leave the cave to feed, all at once, as they do every night."

"Like Barnes." He groaned. "We're too late."

"We have to find his coffin. Then we'll know." She swept her light beam across the boulder-field strewn before them.

He scoffed. "A needle in a barnyard."

"Maybe not." She illuminated the old subway car with her light beam. "Let's check it out."

"I'm right behind you."

Her flashlight shined on the blunt end of the car, a faded letter C above the window, the word "FORDHAM" beside it barely readable. The coupler and steel wheels were rusted and no doubt seized.

Amanda slewed her light to the side door, closed and probably rusted tight. "These old cars are made of wood with a plate-copper covering." She again knelt to her open gym bag.

"How would you know that?"

"Conductor school." She pulled out a prybar. "Hold your light on that door. I'll need both hands for this."

Working as a team, she managed to free one panel of the door and inched it aside enough to make entry. She shoved the gym bag in first, crawled in after it, and then Russell followed. Inside, his flashlight revealed busted lights and broken handholds along the ceiling, stainless steel poles that reached down to the floor, and bench seats with rotted and frayed gray padding.

Amanda opened a compartment with one hand, scythe in the other. Cobwebs.

Russell held the flashlight and gym bag and followed her down the creaking aisle. It was easy to imagine her with clicker punch in hand. "Tickets." The windows on either side of her were blackened with soot and dust, impossible to see out, but in better days gone by, the glory and prestige of the New York City Subway System somehow shown through.

The floor groaned as they moved forward. It seemed darker, damper, and colder with each step until there was a sudden snap, like that of a bone, followed by a crunching and splintering of wood below Amanda's boots. As she sank into a cloud of dust, Russel dropped the gym bag and dove to catch her, missed her but managed to grab the blade of her scythe, jarring her to stop but cutting into his fingers with such force he thought he would never see them again. However, being a vampire, it didn't hurt.

"Russell." Amanda screamed.

"I've got you."

"I can't hold on."

"You have to." He managed to fold his knees under him, then his feet, and finally pulled her back into the subway car.

Now seated on the edge of the jagged flooring, feet still dangling over the abyss, she released her grip on the scythe handle.

He yanked the blade from his flesh, somewhat put aback by the lack of blood, as if his heart wasn't pumping at all.

"What's down there?" she cried.

"I'm all right, Amanda. Don't worry about me." He worked his cut hand into a fist, none the worse for wear.

"Pass me the bag."

He shined his flashlight in her face, saw the terror in her eyes and figured she had more pressing problems to worry about than his little cut. Relieved she wasn't hurt, he passed the gym bag across the chasm.

She fished out a flare, pulled the cord, and dropped it down the hole beneath the subway car. It's blazing glare illuminated a hodgepodge of spikes pointed upward, something that would only be there to guard a forbidden place against intruders.

"The catacombs," she whispered.

In the peripheral of the glow, scattered and tossed caskets could be seen, along with skulls lined up ear to ear and piles of bones.

Russell figured it out. "They didn't want to raze the church to build the subway below it, so the tunnel was dug under it, right through the catacombs. No wonder the ceiling collapsed."

"He's down there. I can feel it." She pulled a coil of climbing rope from her bag. "Tie this end to that pole."

He heard her excited heartbeat, gave the rope a double knot.

She tossed the coil down the hole. "Hold my beer and watch this." A quick test tug then she dropped into the abyss and landed among the knee-high spikes. "Hurry up."

He grabbed the bag and, one handed, slid down the rope to join her.

Winking and spluttering, the flare was about to burn out.

"We don't have much time." She picked up the flare and led with it into the only passageway down there.

The hissing and spitting flame lit walls entirely different than those in the subway tunnels. These walls were hewn from granite by hand and hammer, the chisel marks still evident in the stone. The floor was cobbled and uneven. The air carried the chill of death and the odor of decay.

Deeper and deeper they descended,

past cutouts occupied by hollow-eyed skulls, row upon row, and on down stone steps, lower and lower, past rooms of wooden caskets and sarcophaguses carved from marble. The passageway became narrower, the ceiling lower, and a new obstacle presented itself. Spiders the size of softballs; their web tapestries sticky and unyielding, their bite probably lethal. Only by scythe and blade were they able to proceed. Then, as inevitable as dusk and dawn, the passageway came to an end...at a chamber of pitch black walls—

The flare fizzled out. The sudden darkness was so intense, so oppressive, that not even vampire vision could penetrate its depths.

"Russell?"

"Got it." He flicked on the flashlight. The beam revealed a gathering of corpses, withered and drained, all on bended knees in homage around a coffin made of dark wood and polished to a reflective shine.

"This is it," Amanda breathed.

He tossed her a wooden stake from the gym bag, and took one for himself, which he stabbed behind his belt. "Be careful."

She stepped around each dead soul, all sacrificed to Barnes' unholy nature, and approached the coffin, stake in her fist and a determined snarl on her lips.

Dread gnawed at his guts as he watched her touch the lid, work her way to the center, where she found a handle of carved bone, then looked back at him.

He nodded. Raised the machete as if going to bat for God. Ready.

Please let her be safe.

Amanda threw back the coffin lid then struck downward with the stake, but stopped in mid plunge and just stared into the vampire's bedding of black velvet. "He's not here."

Russell thought he'd peed himself. A presence wafted behind him. His throat tightened. He whirled around but nothing was there...except that creeping mist.

He turned back to Amanda. "He knows we're here."

Wooden stake held high, she pivoted, set her back to the coffin, wooden stake pointed toward the audience of kneeling corpses, *swivel right, swivel left*. "Show yourself, you devil."

"How dare you *ggh* invade my home."

The gravelly voice seemed to come from everywhere at once.

The mist crept around Russell's feet and sifted among the vampire's drained victims, those lost worshipers of the undead.

"And what are you doing here, *ggh,* my spawn? Do you plot with the vampire hunter to kill me, *ggh*?"

"The Midnight Train Murders must stop, Barnes."

"Not until the church is rubble at my feet, *ggh*."

"You may destroy a building," Amanda shouted at empty air, "a parsonage, but not the reverence of people to their God."

Visible only in the spot of light Russell swept about, the mist churned, thickened, and rose to sweep over the drained and shriveled congregation. He recalled how Amanda's form had stepped from a similar mist on the fire escape, and he wondered what abomination would rise from this evil, creeping fog, his likeness, perhaps, or Detective Miles, or an exact replica of Amanda herself? He had to be ready to strike the blade against whatever abhorrence appeared from the now waist-deep haze into which he stepped forward with extreme trepidation.

"Russell. Be careful."

A cold dead hand grabbed his ankle and yanked him off his feet. Down into the mist he fell, crashing face-first into a corpse, its dead eyes and gaping jaws but a flash in the light beam as an echoing screech resounded. He hit the floor. A second cadaver teetered and fell on his chest, pinning him down, as the air above the mist looked to have caught fire, revealing the macabre swamp below the surface, the stoic dead kneeling all around him, the mist thick as water and suddenly unbreathable.

He was drowning.

Fighting panic, he whacked at the corpse with the machete, dispatching its head, an arm, and finally he was free to swim to the surface, a seemingly impossible distance, but once he broke through, he gasped toxic air; he'd emerged into hell's own inferno. Sconces on the chamber walls belched gaseous flames that reached to the ceiling and spread out in every direction.

Amanda's scream echoed around him.

The vampire held her in his clutches from behind, his clawed fingers pressed to her soft, supple throat, his menacing jaws a mere whisper from her ear. "I have waited for this moment so long, *ggh*."

She raised her arm and displayed to Barnes the Celtic cross tattooed on her wrist. "Burn, you devil."

Russell expected smoke to shoot from the vampire's eyes, or maybe his head would burst into flames, but when the monster only laughed, he knew she was in big trouble. "Barnes. Let her go."

His slimy dripping teeth snapped at him. "Say goodbye to your sweety, my spawn, *ggh*."

With one smooth sweep of his claw, Amanda's throat opened in a jagged line, expelling blood and gurgling air.

"No."

Another claw, long and sleek as a saber, suddenly shot out of her stomach, then quickly retracted from her back.

She dropped to her knees, and neck-deep in the mist, her wide and terrorized eyes reflected the flames of this hellhole on earth.

Barnes towered over her, claws dripping blood, as she toppled over, face-first into the mist. His jaws snapped with satisfaction. In that moment of triumph, Russell, in a rage, lunged forward. The machete swept an arc toward the vampire's neck. Barnes had but a split second to turn and raise a clawed paw in defense.

The blade sliced off his hand and continued around to lop off his head, which dropped into the mist, as would a rock into a pond. His decapitated torso fell back into the open coffin, where Russell met him with a wooden stake through the heart.

At that instant, the mist evaporated and the fiery sconces hissed into darkness.

He found the still-glowing flashlight on the floor, grabbed it and rushed to Amanda, now lying in a pool of her own blood. "Amanda."

Her faltering heartbeat sounded faint and far away.

"No. Amanda." He rolled her over on her back.

Blood burbled from her sliced-open throat. Her eyes were but a blank stare in the beam of his flashlight, as were the eyes in Barnes' head lying only a few feet away.

Russell had no time for wailing in anguish, for cursing God, nor voicing his regrets. Her life was spilling out with each labored throb of her heart. In seconds, she would join Barnes in eternity. The thought of losing her to this wretched beast birthed a clear path to insanity. Perhaps it was instinct, or maybe desperation, but something drove him to scoop her up in his arms and put his fangs to her neck, not to suckle, but to bite her, as Barnes had bitten and turned him, by contaminating his blood with some kind of antibody, which he now hoped to pass on to Amanda, to turn her, to save her life, undead as it would be.

With his jaws clamped onto her neck and fangs dug deep, he could taste the coppery smoothness of her blood, feel the weak thump-sputter-thump of her dying heart, and being this close to her brought tears to his eyes, stinging tears that leaked from their wells and trickled down his cheeks in hot rivulets of despair. He wanted to whisper 'I love you' in her ear, and tell her 'I'm sorry' to her face, but he dared not let go of her neck, this connection he had with her, the bridge between life and death so desperately erected in this devil's abode.

Her neck shuddered, followed by a tremor that rippled through her body. The thump-sputter of her heart became a solid thump-thump, and he felt a surge of blood flow around his fangs. Then came a gasp, a whistling flow of air, an expansion of her chest, and a cough. It was only then that he released her and looked into her eyes, now shifting left and right in the glow of his flashlight. He saw that her throat wound had healed and assumed the same about her impaled stomach.

She took a deep breath. "What happened?"

"It's over. He's dead."

"You killed him?"

"In body and spirit, yes, but I'm obliged to make him a legend on paper, and hopefully the church will confess the sins of their founders and then prosper into the future."

"Looks like you got your story, but what about Frank Murphy?"

"The Midnight Train Murders goes to the *Daily Gazette*. Dolan wants me back. I want my credibility back. Screw Frank."

He helped her to her feet.

She stumbled, a little woozy, then straightened. "Something's not right...I feel different. Powerful..." She touched the bite wound on her neck then looked at him with shock-rounded eyes. "What did you do?"

"It was the only way to save you."

"I'm a vampire?"

"And a damn good looking one at that."

"I can't be a vampire. I kill vampires."

He looped his arm around her shoulders. "You didn't kill me."

"But you're different." Her vampire vision revealed Barnes' head on the floor, blank eyes staring up, mouth agape, no sign of his lethal teeth. "Oh, my God."

"He's never coming back."

She looked into the coffin, such a sight, the headless Father Barnes with a stake buried in his chest. "We're not taking any chances." From the gym bag she removed a hammer and a fistful of six-penny nails. She closed the lid and nailed it shut.

"What about his head?"

She lifted it by a gray shank of hair. "Follow me."

He grabbed the gym bag and flashlight and followed her out of the chamber to the coarse spider webs strung about, into which she flung the head and where it stuck suspended above the floor. Within seconds, the giant spiders descended upon it, covered it, and began to feed on its eyes and tongue. Before long, they'd burrow into the ear canals to make quick work of the brain matter within. In a day or two, a hollowed-out skull would be all that remained.

Amanda set her hand on Russell's arm. "Let's go home."

He caressed her chin, admiring her face, her skin so smooth and pale. She was still alive, though undead like himself, and they'd been through a lot together and survived in their own way. That had to mean something for their future. However, one question remained, the age-old one-liner from speakeasies to sports bars:

"Your place or mine?"

About the Author

Born in the Bronx, **Jim Keane** holds a Bachelor of Arts in English from Mount Saint Mary College and has completed many creative writing courses. He's written several short stories and three novels and has more in the works. Jim resides in Westchester, New York, with his family.

Read Jim Keane's short story

Astra's Revenge

Astra's Revenge, (2021, TWB Press)

When a syndicate assassin kills the mother of a circus fortune teller, he can run but he can't hide from Astra's black magic and her crystal ball.

www.twbpress.com/astrasrevenge.html

www.ingramcontent.com/pod-product-compliance
Lightning Source LLC
LaVergne TN
LVHW010059110826
845155LV00028B/414

* 9 7 8 1 9 4 4 0 4 5 8 2 1 *